my

# DRAG TEEN

# DRAG TEEN

## a tale of angst and wigs

### JEFFERY SELF

PUSH

All rights reserved. Published by PUSH, an imprint of Scholastic Inc.,
*Publishers since 1920.* PUSH and associated logos are trademarks and/or
registered trademarks of Scholastic Inc.

The publisher does not have any control over and does not assume any
responsibility for author or third-party websites or their content.

This book is a work of fiction. Names, characters, places, and incidents
are either the product of the author's imagination or are used fictitiously,
and any resemblance to actual persons, living or dead, business estab-
lishments, events, or locales is entirely coincidental.

Library of Congress Cataloging-in-Publication Data available

ISBN 978-0-545-82993-9

10 9 8 7 6 5 4 3 2 1                    16 17 18 19 20

Printed in the U.S.A.    23
First edition, May 2016

Book design by Carol Ly

To Eric Gilliland for the roof, the walls,
and the endless support

# chapter ONE

THIS ISN'T ONE OF THOSE stories about a heartwarming journey toward accepting my cursed homosexual identity. No. First of all, being gay is *far* from a curse. It's more like an extra order of fries at Wendy's because the lady in the window isn't paying attention while she fills your bag. It's awesome.

If there's one thing I've struggled to accept about myself, it's my body. (And that might change, if I stopped eating at Wendy's so much.) Being gay is, in fact, one of the only things I actually like about myself. I've been gay since birth. I've never contemplated the alternative. Literally can't. I have an enormous imagination. But, still, there are limits.

Specifically there are limits if you live in Clearwater, Florida, like I do. Ever been to Clearwater? Spoiler alert: The water isn't that clear. And the town itself? Even murkier.

When my drag teen story started in earnest, I'd been stuck in Clearwater for all seventeen years of my life. But I had big dreams—to maybe someday become a writer or something. I also liked to sing . . . but you can't really say "I dream of growing up to be a singer" without looking like a total lunatic giving a reality show confessional, despite there being zero cameras in sight.

Honestly, though, my dreams never really went much further than the simple hope of getting out of Florida, away from my family, and to somewhere where I could be myself without a single second thought.

This, of course, would require me to figure out who "myself" actually was.

Nobody in my family had ever left Clearwater; none of them had even gone to college. Both my parents grew up in Florida, and their parents grew up in Florida, and their parents, and so on. My great-great-granddad owned some orange groves and had the choice to sell them either to somebody who wanted to open a drive-in movie theater or to some weird guy named Walt Disney. He went with the first option. Which meant that by the time my dad was born, the only money my family had was what they made at the gas station they ran in the middle of town. My granddad passed away when I was really young and left the business to Dad, so I grew up right there pumping gas and cleaning windshields. Up until I was fifteen and discovered cologne, I smelled like gasoline on a daily basis. Now I smelled like whatever scent was on sale at CVS.

I was 100 percent certain that in order for me to get out of Florida and stay out of Florida, I'd need to go off to college. The only problem was that no one in my family had any intention of helping me do such a thing.

Luckily I had another support system that actually believed in the merits of being supportive: Heather, my best friend since first grade. Unlike me, Heather was the kind of loud and opinionated person who would either end up hosting a daytime talk show or being someone's wacky aunt. Still, despite her outward personality and parental advantage, Heather was just as much of a mess as me. Which is why our friendship worked so well. We were the kind of outcasts they don't make teen movies about. Heather was funny, biting, sarcastic, and had a variety of beautiful features, but none of them really went together, and her weight problems were even worse than mine, which meant she turned to her big personality to distract the judgmental eyes of our peers.

We spent most of our time dwelling in the nothingness our town had to offer. The afternoon I'm going to focus on here was like pretty much any other day of our summer. By which I mean, the air was weighted with thick Florida humidity and snarky teenage boredom.

"What should we do today?" I asked. We were in our favorite spot, a little group of old lawn chairs we kept on the roof of the apartment building I'd lived in my whole life. We weren't supposed to be up there, but the landlords didn't complain as long as my parents didn't complain that our ceiling leaked so much we could have opened a water park and charged admission. And then I guess we could have paid to fix the ceiling ourselves.

"Besides pathetically wait for enough time to pass until we can logically eat lunch again?" Heather asked. "What time is Seth getting out of work?"

Seth was my boyfriend. He'd moved to town in ninth grade from Maryland, and we'd been boyfriends from the day we'd met. Seth was all sorts of out of my league, to say the least. His adorable features, perfect body, and wavy blond hair made him look like a cartoon version of an attractive teenager. Plus, he fit in. He was the "cool gay kid" at school, the gay guy everyone wants to be friends with because it gives them the latest must-have fall accessory. Oh, and also because he was genuinely nice and stuff.

I imagined Seth as one of those annoying people who came out of the womb knowing who he was and had never doubted it since. I never saw him worry about what other people might think. But then again, I assumed I wouldn't care that much if I'd never weighed over one hundred fifty pounds and had the kind of abs that just appear for no good reason. This fit into my theory about people with effortless abs and how they must have done something really selfless in a past life—those abs had to be God's way of saying *Psssst . . . Hey, you! I'm sorry.* Even if this theory didn't hold, Seth had the kind of confidence I doubted I'd ever find in myself. I suppose that was one of the many things that drew me to him. To me, the ability to be comfortable enough in your own skin—to actually *like* yourself—was about as foreign as understanding football.

Being a gay kid in this decade of equality and anti-bullying and all that stuff that gay celebrities liked to talk about on TV had so many advantages, but one of the biggest disadvantages was that I couldn't blame why I felt like an outsider on being gay anymore. Gay was in, but that didn't mean that all gay people were. Seth was *very* in. I, however, suspected that I never would be.

My mom's voice howled from downstairs. "JT? Can you come down here?"

She was calling from the kitchen window right below our feet. I could smell the cigarette smoke and hear the incessant yapping of Li'l Biscuit, her eight-year-old Maltese and Chihuahua mix, who hated everyone that wasn't my mom or bacon.

"Coming."

We lived on the top floor of the three-story building, which they had the audacity to call a *penthouse* even though it was still just a two-bedroom apartment with a kitchen the size of most refrigerators. When I got downstairs, leaving Heather to keep watch of the six-pack of Dr Pepper we'd brought up to the roof, I found Mom squeezed in the small space between the countertop and wall, fanning some freshly microwaved Bagel Bites that were bubbling like lava on a smoky paper plate.

"I need you to work tonight," she said. It was not phrased in the form of a question.

She meant work at the gas station, a job I got stuck with countless times even though I rarely got paid.

"Where's Crystal?"

"Her boyfriend's in jail again, and she's got to go to night court."

"But, Mom, I'm hanging out with Seth tonight. It's his only night off all weekend—"

"You tell your friend that you have to help your parents. That gas station is what puts food on our table, JT."

She spoke these words while blowing on the steaming microwaved mini-pizzas she'd purchased on clearance from the Dollar General store with absolutely zero trace of irony.

"First of all, he's not my friend. He's my boyfriend. And he has been for the past three and a half years."

Mom sucked her cigarette and popped a Bagel Bite into her mouth before she even exhaled the cigarette smoke. I winced at the thought of the complicated taste.

"Whatever he is, you're canceling. I really need you tonight."

"Why can't you cover for Crystal?"

"Because your father and I work all day every day to keep a roof over your head, and we deserve some time to relax. That's why." She tossed the unflattering polo shirt at me. "You start at six."

Before I could say another word, Mom was stretched out on the sofa with the plate of Bagel Bites and a whimpering Li'l Biscuit resting on her small hill of a belly.

Sometimes I imagined tossing the gas station uniform in the trash, walking out the door, and never coming back. It wasn't that my parents were horrible people. They didn't hate me, but they didn't appear to be big fans, either. They didn't get me, didn't know any better. They knew only their own world, and had no intention of ever learning anything otherwise. That was the problem with home for me, the lack of otherwise.

When I was a little kid, my grandmother, Nana, would tell me that I was born for big things. Nana was one of the biggest personalities I'd ever met. Loud, the best listener, brutally honest—plus she claimed to have psychic powers. While the only proof of this was the time she predicted my father would have the gout by the time he turned fifty, I always believed that there was something special about Nana. She had seen things, been places, accomplished stuff. And even years after Nana was gone, I still heard her voice in my head, telling me not to give up, to keep trying for something great, to find my otherwise.

First, I had to get wise to just what that "other" might be.

# chapter Two

THE LATE SHIFT AT THE gas station usually meant dealing with people who were pretty drunk. The late shift at the gas station *on a weekend* meant dealing with people who were *epically* drunk. I've never liked drinking, but I guess that's because my parents have always done so much of it. To me, anyone who wants to act stupid and make bad decisions should just go back to being a teenager.

As I stared at the seemingly immobile clock, I realized I was in for a very long, trying shift. But then the bell on the front door jingled, and in walked Seth.

"Yoo-hoo! Anybody home?" he shouted. He was wearing the green tank top with the shape of California on it that I loved. Green was the perfect color on Seth.

"What're you doing here? You're the first sober person I've seen all night. Unless, wait—are you drunk too?"

"How dare you, JT Barnett!" Seth scoffed, playfully putting his hand to his heart. "How could you ever suggest that I, a straight-A student, an accomplished tennis and baseball player, and president of the senior class, would ever risk my perfect record for the frivolity of underage drinking!" He grinned. "Okay. A *little* drunk. And here to see the cutest boy in Clearwater."

He leaned over the counter and kissed me, almost knocking over the display of lighters shaped like guns.

"Gee, thanks. Being the cutest boy in Clearwater is sort of like being the smartest person in, well, Clearwater."

"What time do you get off?"

"Not until midnight. Ugh. One of these days I want to hit the road. Just you and me. Wake up next to each other, order room service, pretend we don't have disgusting morning breath, and cuddle while we eat French toast and watch the third hour of the *Today* show. Doesn't that sound nice?"

It also sounded like the farthest thing from a reality I'd ever know. I'd never stayed in a hotel, let alone ordered room service.

"I come bearing gifts!" He produced a shoe box in an old plastic grocery bag. "I didn't do so great on the wrapping front, but open it!"

"What? Why? It's not my birthday for two months—"

"Just shut up and open it."

I pulled the shoe box out of the bag and shook it. It was way too light to be shoes and not heavy enough to be a million dollars. Then I saw the strand of black hair hanging out of the side and knew *exactly* what it was.

"Seth!"

I opened the box, and inside was a long black wig. It wasn't the nicest wig if you considered yourself a wig aficionado (which I did) but I counted the thought nonetheless.

"I saw it in the window of that thrift shop downtown and immediately knew you needed to have it."

I pulled the wig out of the box and combed my hands through it.

"A thrift shop wig? How punk of you."

Seth knew the way to my heart, which just so happened to be wigs. More than a writer or a singer, I wanted to be a drag queen—or rather a drag *teen*, a term I claimed to have made up (although a quick Google search would have proven otherwise). Unfortunately, following through with my dream made me sick with stage fright. I had only ever performed in drag *once*, and it had *not* gone so well.

But even if I hadn't yet earned my feathered wings, I was still obsessed with drag culture. I suppose it started when I was a kid and stumbled upon that old nineties movie *To Wong Foo, Thanks for Everything! Julie Newmar.* One night when I couldn't sleep I found it on TV and watched the whole thing, the story of three drag queens turning a town upside down by bringing boatloads of wisdom and glamour to a landlocked hamlet. I wanted to know those queens—I wanted them to show up in my town, fix all my problems, and teach me the same kind of wisdom and glamour so I could live life like they lived life.

I confessed this desire to Heather and she very quickly introduced me to *RuPaul's Drag Race*, the reality show where drag queens competed to win money and vodka. On a level that stretched from my gut to my tippy-toes, I understood there was something special about people performing in drag. These queens knew how to find the inner strands of themselves and sew those strands into something fabulous. Usually a dress. They were all so bold, so confident, so strong, so special. I was none of those things and would have settled for just one. That's why I had initially decided to try it, step outside myself and into drag. But that had turned out to be an enormous mistake.

Seth knew this, but still he said, "Put it on."

"Come on, Seth. I told you—I'm not doing it again. Not after—"

"Oh, shut up and let's see how it looks."

Seth was already putting it on my head. I pushed his hands away and took control.

"Okay, well, if I'm going to wear it, at least let me put it on properly." I pushed my bangs back into the netting, pulling the sides down around the corners of my head. I also kept one eye on the door, in case Drunky McNeedgasserson stumbled in and thought I was the funniest thing he'd ever set his beer goggles on. "Well, how do I look?"

Seth cocked his head to the side and grinned.

"I don't think black is your color."

I ripped off the wig and threw it at him.

"Hey!" I said. I was *trying*. "It's not even a good wig, anyway."

"Kidding! I'm kidding!" he pleaded. "There's more to the gift. That was just the first part."

He handed over his iPhone, which was already opened up to a website. I read the headline aloud.

" 'The John Denton Foundation presents the Sixth Annual

Miss Drag Teen Scholarship Pageant.'" I looked up. "What is this?"

"It's another opportunity for you to try performing in drag in a situation that isn't some stupid school talent show."

I handed him back his phone, shaking my head. "You're insane."

"NO! Listen! It's a full scholarship, paid for by some big nonprofit gay charity in New York. With my help and some really hard work, I think we could make it happen."

He passed his phone back to me; I read on.

"'The pageant is seeking high school seniors in need of late-in-the-year financial support for college. Professional performance experience is in no way required. This is a scholarship not for being the greatest drag queen alive but for being the greatest *you* that's hiding inside your heart. Your inner goddess. The *you* you're afraid to show. The *you* that drag can help burst through.'"

I passed back his phone and stared at him as if he'd just turned into a parakeet.

"Seth. Come on. You know what happened last time I tried."

He ignored me and kept reading. "'The most important thing is that you showcase YOU. Prepare a talent portion as well as write and read a personal essay on what drag means to you and how you will follow in the footsteps of award-winning playwright and novelist John Denton and his four rules to live by: finding one's glamour, talent, heart, and soul.'" Seth looked up from his phone, his eyes wide and frustratingly beautiful. "Well?"

"Well, what?" I asked, ready for this whole thing to be over.

"I think you should do it. You're always talking about how you can't find a scholarship that's within reach. I think this could be your perfect ticket out of here."

I let myself indulge the fantasy for a moment: Money for college. No more gas station. An excuse to buy more mascara. A life outside the one I was outgrowing faster and faster every day.

It was everything I wanted.

But then, inevitably, I felt that tug at my gut. The tug that says, "Hey, who do you think you are, Gas Station Boy?"

"But I'm not a drag queen!" I protested. "I love drag queens, but that doesn't mean I can do it. Just like watching the Florida Marlins all the time won't make you a professional football player."

Seth pressed on. "It's baseball—but I see your point. And I also see how wrong your point is. You are totally a drag queen—or at least have major drag queen potential. You were great when you did it in the school talent show. It's not your fault that your audience was made of a collection of inbreds who wouldn't know a good drag queen if she hit them over the head with a platform heel."

He had a point there—the audience of my school talent show had grotesquely underappreciated the art of drag the one and only time I'd tried it. The school talent show had always been a mix of everything Clearwater had to offer—from a Florida version of a Norwegian black metal band to the Peyton sisters' attempt at making their own Cirque du Soleil out of three Hula-Hoops and a bucket of Gatorade. I figured a drag performance would fit right in. Ever since the first time I'd put on a wig in the privacy of my own bedroom, I'd felt so free and it had felt so easy. So I just thought . . . why not?

Unfortunately, on the afternoon of the school talent show, I found out exactly why not.

My doing the talent show *at all* was so out of character for me. I hadn't had much experience getting up in front of strangers onstage. I hadn't had much experience even *talking* to strangers, for that matter. This didn't really hit me until about eleven minutes before I was due onstage. And when it hit me, it wore brass knuckles wrapped around an anvil. *Nervous* and *terrified* didn't even begin to cover it as I sat there, locked in a stall in a bathroom in the backstage area of our school cafe-gym-atorium. I was desperately trying to stop myself from sweating, already feeling beads of makeup-coated perspiration running down from my wig.

My wig, by the way, was terrible. It was a nondescript blue bob I'd bought from the clearance aisle of Kmart, two weeks after Halloween. Also, I was wearing this big, puffy dress that made me look like I was being swallowed by yellow cotton candy, or had fallen feetfirst into a freshly peed-on mound of snow. I had managed to squeeze my feet into a pair of Heather's heels but my feet were at least three sizes too big. It had never occurred to me that walking in heels would be somehow different from the shoes I was used to wearing. *Graceful* has never been a word you immediately pinned to my physical prowess; a flailing, tumbling human version of Jenga was a tad closer to accuracy. The heels only served to make matters worse. I felt like I was attempting to balance all of my weight (a number that is absolutely none of your business) on two shaky pencils, while my crammed-in toes felt like they were bound together with a billion of those little rubber bands they use to torture people with orthodontia.

Needless to say, I was a wreck.

I had looked at the running order and was counting down to my turn like a prisoner awaiting execution. I had exactly two performances until I had to walk the plank—or, rather, perform. The bathroom stall was hot, and not helping my sweaty makeup in the least, so I figured it was now or never. On top of being freaked out, I was also mad at myself for being so freaked out. I mean, sure, being a teenage boy at his school talent show in yellow taffeta could feel a bit unnerving, but it was more than that. It had felt so exciting when I'd first thought about it, the idea of stepping outside of myself into this whole other persona and having nothing to lose. But now I was betraying myself. Like I'd invested so much of my heart into it, into the idea of feeling beautiful and important and talented, that the very real and likely possibility that it would go horribly wrong was already looming over me like an avalanche of self-loathing about to crash down.

I clicked open the bathroom stall and took my first few wobbly steps, grasping on to the automatic hand dryer for balance. It immediately, and very loudly, turned itself on, which took me by such surprise that I almost fell into the trash can.

I checked myself in the mirror one last time. My makeup was far from perfect but I'd done the best I could. I adjusted my wig, wishing it was a nicer and more expensive, like the wigs on *Drag Race*. Then, like a contestant on *Drag Race*, I took a deep breath and opened the door to the stage. A group of sophomore girls were singing a mostly off-key rendition of an already not-so-on-key Ariana Grande song and it was going over super well, the audience cheering and whistling along. I was lost in thought, thinking about how much easier it would have been for me to do something simple, like stay home, watch *House Hunters International*, and not compete in the school talent show at all. Then I snapped back to my non-alternate reality and realized that everyone backstage was staring at me. They weren't making faces, or laughing, or anything flat-out mean . . . but they couldn't stop staring, blankly, the way you stare when you find something bizarre in a place you don't expect to find something bizarre. Like when there's a dead opossum in a pool skimmer and you just sorta stare at it for a second like, *Hm, I wonder what THAT is about* before getting a net and wrestling it out.

Just as I was coming to terms with this silent humiliation, I heard the show's host, Mrs. Patterson, the school drama teacher whose claim to fame was that she'd had two lines in an episode of the short-lived *Law & Order: Key West*. As she began to introduce me, I realized she couldn't have cared less about what I, or anyone else for that matter, was going to do—she was too focused on her own role as host. I had a strong inkling that the only reason we had a school talent show at all was so Mrs. Patterson could put on a nice gown and talk on a wireless microphone for two and a half hours.

"And now . . . JT Barnett!"

Her voice boomed from the scratchy monitor in the wings. I walked toward the stage, and felt I was walking into the oft-discussed posthumous light. My eyes took a while to adjust from the extreme contrast between the dim backstage and the brightness onstage. I wondered, briefly, how Beyoncé pulled it off during her concerts, even managing to DANCE while stage-blind. I thought I might step off the stage any second as my blurry vision adjusted, looking much more drunk than "Drunk in Love."

The room was mostly quiet as I made my way to center stage. There were a few murmurs and coughs, a few muffled laughs and gasps from people who acted like they'd never seen a boy in a dress before. I was trying to ignore it, telling myself to focus on the song, focus on the performance. I couldn't see the audience at all, which was a blessing, but I wished I could at least catch a quick glimpse of Seth and Heather to boost my spirits. Instead, I reminded myself that they were out there and I knew they were cheering me on. That managed to boost my spirits enough to start as someone backstage hit play.

I was going to be singing "Part of Your World" from *The Little Mermaid*—a song that was definitely in the top five of gay gay gay. I didn't mind that, mainly because I'd always loved the song and I knew I sang it really well. (Actually, most people could do that song really well. Even Heather sounded pretty on that song, and next to my dad and Cameron Diaz, she was probably the worst singer of all time.)

The song began, and I made up my mind to give it my all. I told myself that I did in fact look pretty no matter how much my shaky nerves were trying to convince me otherwise. I planted my heels firmly on the ground and unleashed my voice from the seashell inside of me. It felt good.

I got through about a third of the song before I heard it—*fag* or another of those trivial slurs ignorant people use as if they matter. I didn't care. When someone calls a teenage boy in a dress, singing a song from *The Little Mermaid*, a fag, their obviousness doesn't garner a response. Name-calling didn't bother me—I had half expected it, and I wasn't going to let it ruin everything. I kept going.

The name-calling got a little worse, a few more stupid snickering teenage-boy voices echoing throughout the room. I could feel the tension building. Why was no one stopping them? Where were the teachers?

When I got to the midsection, which was the part where I could really unleash my inner Ariel to its best effect, there was a loud buzz from the speakers and then the sound stopped cold. Much to my horror, the note I was reaching for instead fell under the sea. I pulled back from the mic as if it had given me an electric shock—and nearly teetered over on my heels. This teeter got plenty of titters. Phones came out, and the audience immediately started muttering and Instagramming.

And me?

I.

Just.

Stood.

There.

Mrs. Patterson came onstage so fast you would have thought someone was offering her a third line on *Law & Order: Key West*. In a grave tone usually reserved for presidential assassinations, she said there'd been a brief problem with the sound equipment but that it was being fixed and would be back in no time.

"In the meantime," she said, "perhaps JT would like to finish his song a cappella. What do you think?"

She should have never given them an option. There was some applause. I vaguely thought I heard Seth and Heather cheer. But the bullies were louder, taking Mrs. Patterson's question as an invitation to boo. At first it was only five or so of them, but then it was ten, then twenty. Then it felt like the entire school had joined in. I was paralyzed, as if each boo was another punch in the gut. Finally I found the energy to rip off my wig and run off the stage. Mrs. Patterson tried to stop me, but only barely. I think she was excited to fill the time with a story about the time she met Burt Reynolds, at least until the sound went back on.

I tried to push my way back to the bathroom stall, past the guys backstage who were laughing and whispering, not so quietly, cruel insults about my body and my voice. I wished they had called me another gay slur—those I could take, those were silly—but the other stuff . . . it actually hurt. I stayed in the bathroom stall until the talent show was over and I was sure that every single person had left the backstage hallway.

When you put yourself out there, like I had done, and people take that and crap all over it, they manage to make the horribly mean voices in your head that say you're not good at anything sound as rational and correct as you fear they are. Even as I stood there with my supportive boyfriend, even as he was saying all the right things, he didn't have a chance against the voices in my head.

"Seth," I said, "I don't think this is for me. I really appreciate your thinking of me, but no."

Seth dramatically slapped the countertop, knocking over the age-requirement sign for buying cigarettes.

"Why?" he challenged. "Give me one reason why not."

*Just one?* I thought, cataloging the talent show, the bathroom stall, the boos, the ugly yellow dress; the look of pity from everyone in the backstage hallway flashed in my head like one of those old flip-books.

But then I thought—*Oh yeah. I can boil it down to just one.*

"Okay," I said. "How about this? I'm *not good enough.*"

"But you are!"

"But I'm not, Seth! I'm really not."

Seth put his phone back in his pocket, shaking his head. "Fine. Forget it. I was trying to help, but you know what, JT? None of us will ever be able to help you until you decide to let us."

He was saying, *Here, take some help,* and I was hearing, *You are even failing at being a failure—how sad is that?* So I struck back.

"Why don't you find another charity, then?" I said. "Take this third-hand knockoff of a Cher wig and send it to some starving child in some part of the world where they don't have wigs!"

Seth headed over to the door. "I've got to get going."

But I didn't want him to leave like that. He was always trying to build me up, and I hated myself for how much I refused to let him.

"Seth. Wait."

He stopped, took a deep breath, and walked back over to the counter. He kissed me, sweetly and briefly.

"You know what I want?" he said. "For your sake? I want you to open your eyes. You know I love you, right?"

I nodded.

"And you love me?"

I nodded again.

"Okay. Then I wish that you could embrace all of that. All of you and me."

"And that means me doing a drag pageant?"

"No. It means allowing yourself to go after what you want, even if you're afraid. It means embracing yourself enough that you allow me to fully embrace you too."

I came out from around the counter. There was something too weird about fighting over a counter full of discounted candy bars and air fresheners.

"Hey." I pulled Seth into me. He smelled so wonderful, so clean, so Seth. "I think you're incredible."

Seth looked up at me, his chin resting in that little indention in my chest he always called his spot.

"You're not getting out of this that easy. I just want you to loosen up. Be who you are, one hundred percent. And see how great you are."

I thought about how much I beat myself up about my love handles and my saggy butt anytime I saw someone like Channing Tatum on TV. I thought about how uncool I felt all the time, every day, as far back as I could remember. I thought about how every time a hot guy posted a gym selfie on Instagram it made me dizzy with envy. I thought about how much I wondered why Seth would want to be with someone like me. And I thought about how little I actually believed I'd ever do anything but pump gas.

I cleared my throat and swallowed my lack of pride.

"I'll work on it."

"You felt comfortable and proud of yourself once. I saw you getting ready for the talent show. You were so . . . you. Don't forget that."

"Yeah, and I went straight from that to worst I've ever felt about myself, standing up there in front of everybody, being a loser."

I could tell by how red his ears were getting that Seth was annoyed. They always did that.

Now they were essentially glowing.

"You aren't a loser, JT," he said. "Try to convince yourself of that? Please? For me?"

"Okay," I said.

But I wasn't sure I meant it.

# chapter THREE

I HATE TESTS. I GUESS everyone does. I could never trust a person who actually *likes* tests. The weird thing is that tests are something you mostly only have to worry about when you're a kid. After college, tests are basically done. Which is one of the many reasons I think life doesn't really start until after these horrible teenage years are officially over.

One way for me to avoid Seth's drag teen proposal was to find another way to afford college. To that end, I decided to take the Kingston National Bank Academic Scholarship exam. It took place early on a Saturday morning, the weirdest time to be inside a school. There were about thirty of us in the classroom taking the exam, which was basically an SAT rip-off. Long essay prompts, multiple choice questions, and, the worst part of all, lots of math problems. One of my biggest goals for when I grew up was to never have to do math problems *ever* again. I just had to get through these, I told myself, and I could get a scholarship, go off to college, and get a job that didn't leave me smelling like unleaded gasoline. And when I needed to do math, there would be apps for it.

I'd always wanted to write. I used to write in a journal every night, starting in second grade. The early entries were silly stuff—lists of food I ate that day, a poem about how pooping works, whatever. But they got deeper as I got older, and I wished so badly I still had them. My mother threw them out because they were taking up too much shelf space that she needed for the dolls she collected from the Home Shopping Network. She swore they would someday be worth the millions of dollars that would pay for retirement somewhere exotic, like Tampa.

"Pencils down," Mrs. Bogart, a birdlike woman who worked in the school's office, instructed at the end of the exam. "We will announce the three selected students first thing Monday morning."

The idea of waiting until Monday was nauseating. This was my last shot. The last possible scholarship, really. I'd applied for each one I could find—even one for Native American students, because my great-great-great-grandmother's ex-husband may or may not have been part Cherokee. My grade point average wasn't horrible but my math scores barred me from the Hope Scholarship and anything else based on academic merit. Other than that, I had no real skills (i.e., sports) to get me into a school's good financial graces. To make matters even more frustrating, I'd applied and gotten into a few schools, and some of them were even ones I wanted to go to. However, the situation was simple: Unless my name was one of the three called out on Monday, the next year of my life would be the start of a really depressing future stuck in Clearwater. I'd have to distract myself until Monday. So I did what I always did when I needed to clear my mind. I went for a long drive with Heather and Seth.

"Doesn't it feel like they play the same five songs on the radio over and over, all day long?" Heather asked, not so much as a question but as a declaration of our times.

"Do you think it's because there are only five good songs out at a time?" Seth fired from the backseat, his face lit in the glow of his iPhone like somebody telling a campfire ghost story.

"No," Heather snapped. "There are way more than five good songs out at a time. But the world is full of basic people like you, who don't hear about a song unless it's from somebody with three million followers on Twitter."

We were taking our usual drive down the coast, along the Gulf of Mexico. It's pretty, even though no matter how long we drove, we still ended up in Florida. No matter how sick of Florida I got, I could never get sick of the water at night. I suspected this was the case with all oceans. I'd only seen the Atlantic a few times, since it was on the other side of the state, but I still felt there was something magical about bodies of water that large, something that said there's more than you and me, more than college scholarships, more than grim futures at gas stations. Sometimes I felt like the rest of the world was getting to see the big picture, and that I was the only one missing out. But the ocean? The ocean was something none of us would ever understand, and that was oddly comforting.

"How do you think the exam went?" Heather asked, her Bette Davis eyes on the road.

I had told Seth earlier in the day that I didn't want to talk about the exam, and he was supposed to have relayed this message to Heather. Odds were good that he had, and that she was blithely ignoring it.

"I'd really rather not—"

Seth joined in, egging me on. "I mean, this is huge for you. This is basically your last shot at a scholarship, at college, at a future. This is major, unless of course you were to consider *my* idea—"

"We get it." I turned up the radio, hoping to drown out both Heather and Seth, but Heather lowered the volume again.

"You can talk to us, JT," Seth pushed on. "We're your friends. Keeping things bottled up all the time sucks. Believe me, I know."

"What does *that* mean?" I asked.

"Nothing. Never mind," Seth said after an uncomfortable beat of silence.

"Hot dogs!" Heather shouted as she jerked the car into the parking lot of Hal's, the hot dog stand that had been on the side of the highway for as long as I could remember. It was one of those places that looked really cool without knowing it. Tacky Christmas lights hung between palm trees over a patch of weathered old picnic tables, a huge grill, a little yellow shack, and the omnipresent aroma of hot dogs. The place was always crowded because one of those TV shows about food said Hal's served the best hot dog in Florida, and they were right.

We ordered at the counter. All of the hot dogs were named after famous people from Florida. As much as I hate to admit it, I ordered the Brittany Snow. What can I say? I like coleslaw.

We made our way over to a table in the corner, across from a cluster of cute guys. They went to our school but were the kind of popular kids whose names I never could have learned even if I'd tried. The kind of kids who probably had been there laughing at me during the school talent show.

"Those guys go to our school, don't they?" Seth said between bites of his Gloria Estefan Dog. "Heather, don't you know the one in the blue?"

Heather looked over her shoulder at the very cute boy in a blue T-shirt across the way. "Yeah. Patrick Eberhart. He lives down the street from me. I used to swim in his pool when we were little kids."

"Go talk to him." Seth nudged her with his elbow. "He's really cute and he keeps looking over at you."

"I haven't talked to him in forever. He probably doesn't even remember me."

"You grew up down the street from him. It's not like that was fifty years ago. Of course he remembers you. Don't you think he's cute?"

Heather looked over her shoulder again.

"Yeah."

"Well then. GO!" Seth tossed one of his fries at her, which landed in her frizzy hair.

"Right. The weirdest and fattest girl in school goes to talk to one of the popular guys at her favorite hot dog stand. That's a movie I do NOT want to see. Much less be a part of."

"Do it! I demand it! And it's my birthday next month." Seth never took no for an answer.

"Oh sure, because that makes sense."

"No, Heather. You owe it to yourself. Be bold. Be brave. It's like I'm always telling JT. Ditch the whole self-hating BS and just live."

"Seth, leave her alone. If she doesn't want—" I tried to protest, but he wasn't giving up that easy.

"Heather, you're beautiful. The world is full of different kinds of beauty. Sure, you don't look like those cookie-cutter popular girls, but who cares? You look like *you*, and that's better than being a cookie cutter."

Heather was quiet for a moment, a rare phenomenon. Sometimes it seemed like she was afraid of silence. Heather always dominated the conversation, no matter who she was talking to. I think that was one of the reasons I loved her, because I never had to worry about saying something interesting.

The boy in the blue shirt must have noticed us looking at him. Everyone at his table was very aware of us, which was the last thing I wanted.

"Heather," I said, "you don't have to do anything you don't want to do. Let's just go—"

"You know what? He's right," Heather said, smoothing her frizzy hair and adjusting her oversize sweater. "What do I have to lose? How do I look?"

The truth was that Heather looked bizarre against the back-drop of Clearwater, no matter where she went. Walking down the street in a big city, Heather would have made perfect sense, maybe even looked fashion-forward and hip. But to people in Clearwater she looked like a wacky bag lady with a penchant for doughnuts.

"Beautiful," Seth said.

Before I could respond, Heather was marching over to the picnic table of popular guys. Seth watched her go, then turned back to me. "You should encourage her more."

"Huh?"

"You always let her stand back, the way you do. She should step out on her own and shine."

"What does that even mean?"

"You both need a dose of confidence. You let her doubt herself. And she lets you. I see it. It's like the drag pageant scholarship—"

I gave him a look that said *Shut up or I will kill you*. He pretended not to notice.

"I just don't want you to be stuck here. I know that you don't either. It kills me to imagine me and Heather getting to graduate and go off to begin our lives while you have to stay in Clearwater to fend for yourself."

It was the first time I'd ever heard Seth talk about his future without me, and the first time I felt what it did to my heart. I'd always fantasized that Seth, Heather, and I would move off to New York together, get a dumpy yet charming apartment, work at bad jobs we'd love to complain about, and use that as a home base to seek out our dreams.

"Well, you don't know where you'll go," I pointed out. "The other day you said you were still considering going to Florida State. Maybe if I don't get a scholarship, I can apply for financial aid and get in-state tuition or something. Right?"

Seth looked at me blankly. Carefully, he said, "I thought you knew I had changed my mind. I can't just turn down offers from places like Ithaca or Emerson."

"So you're definitely going to leave Florida after graduation?"

"I don't think this is the right time or place to have this conversation. All I'm saying is that Heather, like you, needs to be more confident, and you should be encouraging her, while you encourage yourself."

Seth might have seemed like just another pretty, charming boy with perfectly wavy hair, but he was really smart. And as much as I hated to admit it, he was right. If I couldn't be confident in myself, how could I help my best friend be confident in herself? But Heather was already headed back over to us, with her head planted firmly down.

"Let's go," she said stiffly, grabbing her purse.

"How did it—"

She snapped back at Seth, "Let's just go! Okay?"

We drove back to the drone of today's latest pop songs whispering quietly on the radio.

"So," I tentatively offered.

Heather kept staring at the passing darkness along the road.

"So?" she repeated back to me, with a hefty dose of attitude that eventually managed to say, *I know you want to talk about what just happened but I'm not going to so if you're going to insist on trying to get me to talk then I'm going to be forced to murder you.*

Needless to say, I shut up.

We dropped Seth at his house and I kissed him good-night. It felt like one of those distracted kisses where both of you are in completely different headspaces but kissing because that's what you're supposed to do when you're boyfriends saying good-bye to each other. He knew I wanted to talk more about his future and mine; he knew how insecure I was about him going off to college and our attempting to have some sort of long-distance relationship. I was giving myself a migraine.

Heather drove me across town to my neighborhood. A far cry from the picturesque cul-de-sac Seth called home. As she pulled up to the apartment building, we were both quiet. I could see the sadness in her eyes and she could see the worry in mine.

"Will you please just tell me whether or not you're okay?" I asked, finally.

It was dark inside the car, but I could tell she wasn't smiling.

"I'm fine."

Normally, I would have stopped here. But maybe Seth was right. Maybe I needed to be a better friend, and part of that meant pushing a little harder. So instead of letting it go, I said, "You sure? You don't look any definition of fine that I'm familiar with."

Heather sighed. "That guy I grew up with? Patrick from the hot dog stand? Yeah, he wasn't trying to flirt with me. When I got over there, he and his friends told me they should've asked me to order for them, because I looked like the place's best customer."

"WHAT?! Those assholes. You know that you're—"

"Stop."

Heather was flustered and attempting to hide how truly upset she was. She sighed again, and this time the sigh seemed to contain the entire state of Florida.

"We're gonna get out of here someday, right? And get somewhere where we fit in? Right?"

I fell silent because I really wasn't sure and I didn't want to lie to her. Maybe I wouldn't pass that scholarship test; maybe I wouldn't get my ticket to my otherwise; maybe I'd be stuck in Florida, without Seth, without Heather.

"Seth's definitely going somewhere out of state," I said.

"Are you sure?" From the look on her face, I could tell she wasn't fronting—he hadn't told her, either.

"Yeah. He told me so, at Hal's."

Heather squeezed my shoulder. "You will too—"

"But what if he goes somewhere for smart, fancy people? What then?"

Heather shrugged. "Then you'll go somewhere for interesting, messy people." She cracked a smile, then added, "Without Seth."

I didn't want to hear this. "Stop. Sorry I brought this up at all."

She grabbed my knee. "Remember, he's your first boyfriend, JT. We're both seventeen."

"So?"

"So . . . does anybody actually end up with their first boyfriend?"

I had never thought about this before and I suddenly felt scared. Pit-of-the-stomach scared.

Heather saw what she'd done and tried to backpedal. "Hey, sorry. Don't let that upset you. I was just trying to put things in perspective. Forget I said anything. Okay?"

I nodded, though I knew how my brain worked. If there was something to worry about, I would worry about it until I was physically incapable of worrying anymore. The best I could do right now was attempt to change the subject. Instead of thinking about Seth, I'd focus on me and Heather.

"Let's make a pact," I said. "You and me. No matter what happens, we'll get out of here someday. Go far away from Florida. We'll find a place where we aren't the freaks, but just the people."

I imagined this as I said it. I imagined us in some big city where everybody was just as weird as us, if not weirder.

"Someday soon."

"Yes," I promised, as much to myself as to her. "Someday soon."

# chapter **FOUR**

"AND WITHOUT FURTHER ADO . . ."

Principal Kelly's voice sounded like Darth Vader through the school's crappy intercom system.

"The three scholarship winners are . . ."

My heart was pounding so hard I worried it might pound right out of my chest and onto the floor of the science lab.

"Reese Firstman."

Okay, that wasn't a surprise. Reese was one of those people who only had bad grades because she was too smart to actually care about high school. She probably hadn't even studied for the scholarship exam.

"James Hansen."

Okay, one left.

*Please say my name. Please say my name.*

"And . . ."

My throat tightened.

"Mary Soria."

The pounding suddenly stopped. I began to feel that salty weight that says, *You're gonna cry and you can either do it where you are, in this case a high school science lab, or get to the bathroom as fast as you freaking can, bitch.* I didn't even raise my hand. I just slipped out the back and bounded my way to the boys' room. As soon as the door swung shut behind me, tears poured out. So did the heavy breathing I get when I'm overwhelmed with how bad I feel.

*No scholarships, no college.* The story was over.

I was officially stuck in Clearwater.

The bathroom door burst open and Heather barreled in.

"I came as fast as I could!" She pulled me into her soft chest. What Heather lacked in confidence she made up for in boob size.

"You can't be in here, Heather." My voice was muffled so far into her cleavage it almost echoed.

"Look at me." She pulled me away and stared into my eyes. "Screw them. Screw that scholarship."

"That's easy for you to say. You're not the one who just had his last shot taken away."

"It can't possibly be your last shot. There are billions of scholarships out there."

"I've tried, Heather. I've Googled into the depths of the Internet. I can't afford any more application fees. I have no skills."

Heather smacked me on the cheek.

"Don't you ever say that again. You're a wonderful person! A wonderful singer! A wonderful writer. A gorgeously talented writer. You just happen to have insanely bad grades."

"Thanks."

"Like really bad. Like how did they get so bad to begin with? How do you let yourself go like that—"

"Okay. I get it."

Heather began pacing, the wheels of her brain spinning, as Seth rushed in.

"Sorry it took me so long," he said. "My teacher wouldn't let me leave until he finished telling us why the world will probably be destroyed by the time we're fifty. How are you?"

"It didn't take fifty years for my world to be destroyed—only seventeen."

Instead of trying to persuade me otherwise—it wouldn't have worked—Seth pulled me in and kissed my lips. He was wearing Dr Pepper ChapStick. It helped me smile.

"What are you doing in the guys' bathroom?" Seth asked Heather.

She snorted. "Please. Save it. I'm more of a man than most of the guys at this school."

Seth nodded understandingly. She had a point.

"Okay," she said with some urgency. "Here's what we're going to do. We're going to spend tonight researching scholarships."

"But I told you, I've already—"

Heather cut me off, relentless. "What about scholarships that play the gay card? Can't you just write to that guy who played Spock in the new Star Trek movies, and see if he'll pay for you to go to college? Or Ellen? She's always giving gay people money on her show."

Something twinkled in Seth's eyes. "Well. I found

*something* . . . but JT won't even consider it." As he said this, he casually played with a strand of his perfect hair. Irresistible jerk.

"Does he have to pretend to be Chinese? I already looked into that one, and he is NOT conversant in the Mandarin language."

"No," I said, "his idea is completely absurd and complicated."

"It's a drag pageant!" Seth exclaimed. "It basically works like a beauty pageant for teenage drag queens and the winner gets a full scholarship!" Seth was doing his best sales pitch and Heather was hanging on his every word.

"What? JT!" she exclaimed. "That sounds perfect! You love drag queens!"

"That doesn't mean I can be one myself. I love old Jessica Lange movies too but that doesn't mean I have any right to be in one!"

Heather ignored me and plowed on. "Is this about what happened last time? That was a dumb school talent show. Of course they didn't get you—"

Now it was my turn to interrupt with a reality check. "They didn't just *not* get me. They booed and laughed at me!"

"Okay, fine. You were a teenage boy performing at his high school in drag—what did you expect? This is different. This is where we aren't the freaks. Where is it located?"

"New York!" Seth squealed with excitement. "We've GOT to go!"

They were drinking the Kool-Aid of this idea way too fast—and it wasn't kool, and it didn't particularly aid me. "You guys, come on!" I protested. "We can't just up and run off to New York for some pageant. Who do you think we are?"

Heather passionately pulled me toward her so we were face-to-face.

"Fine," she said. "It's the last thing you want to do again . . . but who cares? You need a scholarship and they have one to give. You can't give up on something you were so excited about just because it went poorly the first time."

It *went poorly.* That was one way of putting it. Another way would have been: *Everyone watching literally LAUGHED AT ME, BOOED, SHOUTED INSULTS. They were all so mean, so vicious, so cruel. It was like the final scene in* Carrie *but without pig's blood and with way more eyeliner.*

I couldn't put myself through that again.

"You guys. I don't think—"

Seth placed his soft hand on my shoulder. "It's a full scholarship. All four years. A full ride, JT."

Seth's eyes weren't just sparkling now; they were drilling into me. Did he see something I didn't? Was he right? If I tried again, could there be even a tiny chance I could actually do it? Did he actually think I could—

The door flew open and Mr. Garcia bounded in.

"Young lady, you have no business in here. All of you, back to class. Right now. GO!"

As we parted ways outside the bathroom door, Seth looked over his shoulder at me and smiled. Heather grabbed my hand, and as she squeezed it, she whispered, "Think about it, JT. I believe in you."

# chapter **Five**

ONCE IT WAS IN THERE, I couldn't get the idea out of my head.

Was I actually considering doing it again? After my one drag experience, I'd vowed I'd never do it again, but could I muster up the audacity to change my own mind? Could I ignore the horrible memories? If my life were a musical, this particular moment would've made a really good character-driven ballad about hope and fear that would come back as a reprise in the second act to mean something entirely different. The kind of show tune people would sing, most frequently off-key, in auditions.

Also there was the matter of originality and pride. I was far from original, and the last time I'd actually felt proud was when I first saw myself fully in drag. Before the competition, before the humiliation; I felt wonderful, but not for long. And the last time I remembered feeling proud before that was when I went to a sleepover in fourth grade and *didn't* wet the bed.

My curiosity was getting the better of me, so later that night I Googled more about the pageant. The information online made it clear that while it was a "beauty pageant," it wasn't meant in the traditional Miss America sense. The whole idea of beauty not being what we look like but who we are was definitely a comforting thing to remember.

There was no swimsuit competition, thank God. But there was an opening number where each contestant would be introduced, a talent portion, an interview portion, and then the essay performance.

I had no talent. Sure, I enjoyed singing, alone in my room, but that didn't make it a *talent*. Nowadays you had to sing while ice-skating through a ring of burning cars or be famous for zero reason on Vine in order to be called talented.

And then there was the whole *competition taking place in New York* thing. I was in Florida, which meant it wasn't exactly a bus ride across town. I had a hundred and ten dollars saved up in a sock in my dresser, but that was all I had to my name. That wouldn't even get me a one-way plane ticket. Asking my parents was out of the question, especially because they believed that anything you needed in life could be found at Walmart, and if Walmart didn't have it, then you could probably live without it.

Who was this John Denton of the John Denton Memorial Foundation, anyway? According to the information online, he had been a big playwright in New York during the seventies and eighties. He was some kind of cult icon who had no family and had chosen to leave his entire estate to this foundation in hopes of, as he put it, "helping to empower and strengthen the minds and confidence of queer youth in the way it took me an entire life to do for myself."

I wondered what it was that had finally strengthened the confidence of this John Denton character, what finally made him feel comfortable in his own skin, and if it was even possible for me to find that in myself at all.

The competition was scheduled for the first week of April, which was our school's spring break. A trip to New York for spring break would be like a dream come true. But as with all of my dreams, I inevitably had to wake up and smell the coffee—or, in my case, the gasoline.

There was absolutely no way it could happen.

My phone rang—it was Seth. Like he had spies in my mind to tip him off that I was thinking about his idea.

"Hello?" I answered.

"Hi. Are you still mad at me?"

"I was never mad at you."

He chuckled his dumb little chuckle that only he could make cute.

"I know. I'm just calling to say hey."

"I was just on the website for the scholarship, actually. Did you know John Denton was some obscure playwright who left his money to this foundation to help gay kids?"

"I see *someone's* been doing his research."

"Isn't it crazy to think about how when somebody like John Denton was a kid, the very word *gay* was considered so taboo he couldn't have even said it?" I asked. I had never lived in a world where *gay* wasn't at the very least the description of a wacky next-door neighbor on a TV show. Sure, it wasn't always easy to be gay in Clearwater, Florida, but it wasn't anything like someone like John Denton would have experienced. Gay people were everywhere now and some of them were getting married and having kids, to a degree that John Denton probably wouldn't have been able to wrap his head around. Sure, I was insecure about almost everything, but at least I had the freedom to be proud of being a gay person, even if I wasn't wild about the person part.

"Yeah," Seth said. "Crazy, huh? And to think after his struggles he still left this amazing legacy for someone like you and you don't even want to try to take it."

"Seth," I said, flat and edgy, the way I always did when I was over a particular subject.

"I just want you to let go of what you felt before. We all have to do that once in a while; we all just have to move on from something that made us feel bad about ourselves sometimes. You can't hold on to it."

"Oh yeah. When was the last time *you* had to let go of something that made you feel bad?"

Seth was uncharacteristically quiet on the other end, as if I'd upset him.

"You still there?"

He brushed off the whole conversation with a laugh and said he had to run, but before he hung up he told me he loved me no matter what and would always be there to believe in me. I wondered why, even in modern times, even with all that had changed since somebody like John Denton was around, even with a gorgeous boy telling me he loved me . . . I still couldn't face an opportunity that, sure, scared me, but also excited me in a way

I was just too scared to admit to myself or anyone else. I wondered what John Denton would say.

Later that night, I ate dinner in front of the TV, which was tuned in to the Home Shopping Network because Mom was in control of the remote. A woman was selling sixty-dollar snow boots people could pay for in five installments. With a sleeping Li'l Biscuit in her lap, Mom was on the phone, reading her credit card number to the operator on the other end of the line. Dad came in, tired as always, dirty as always, and with a beer in his hand as always.

"Four-five-five-four . . . seven-nine-two . . ." Mom squinted at her Visa.

"What's she doing?" Dad asked, plopping into the ratty old recliner only he was allowed to sit in.

"Ordering boots, I think." I bit down on the frozen burrito Mom had "cooked" for dinner, the center still ice-cold.

"What the— Debby! Hang up that phone right now!"

Mom waved her hand at him and moved on to the expiration date.

Dad continued to huff and puff but Mom just talked over him. Finally he grabbed the phone and hung it up before she could get to the security code.

"Hey! Those snow boots are on sale!"

"What the hell do you need snow boots for?" Dad tossed the phone onto the couch beside me. "We live in Florida!"

Mom groaned as she lit a cigarette and took a deep, long drag, which was followed by a deep, long cough.

"We need to save some money. JT is graduating this year and

we gotta think about the future," Dad said, taking off his shoe. The odor of his foot filled the room—an odor that could have peeled paint off of a car.

I perked up. It was the first time Dad had ever used *JT* and *future* in the same sentence. I was actually surprised he remembered it was my senior year.

"Right, son? It's about time we start thinking about your education."

I couldn't believe it. Dad had *never* talked about my education, except the one time he got mad at me for reading too often.

"I picked this up for you today." Dad slapped a brochure onto the coffee table, a cloud of dust billowing in its wake. I looked down.

*Clearwater Technical School Auto Repair Department.*

"I figure you ought to start taking classes this summer, get a jump start on the training, and maybe we can open a little shop for ya in that old garage behind the gas station. Buddy of mine says the mechanical industry is really booming."

I had thought, for a moment, that my father was approaching an understanding of what I wanted.

Now, not so much.


I was sure that auto repair classes at the technical college would have been awesome for some other teenager, someone whose passion lay under the hood. I knew those guys existed. My dad had been one of them. But this wasn't exactly what I imagined for my own education. I hated cars almost as much as I hated living in Clearwater.

"Dad, I don't think I'm—"

He cut me off. "I know what you're gonna say, but you can learn. Apparently it ain't that hard. You know Pooter down at the Reichen Auto Body Shop? He's dumb as a brick. But give that guy a screwed-up engine, and he'll have it fixed quicker than you could drive to Pizza Hut and back."

I couldn't believe what I was hearing. My father was comparing my future to that of a man named Pooter.

"I'm not going to auto repair school. I'm just not. Save your money. Let Mom buy those snow boots. I want to go to college."

Dad's face flushed, the way it always did when he got mad or ate red meat.

"I think he's right," Mom said, reaching for the phone. "I *should* order those boots."

Dad grabbed the phone away from her.

"Look, there's nothing wrong with technical college or auto repair or whatever," I told him, "but that's just not what I want, okay? I want to do something different. I want to live in different places. I want to see the world and be somebody." I was on the verge of tears, but I fought them back.

"You ungrateful little son of a—"

Dad stopped himself, lit a cigarette from the box on the coffee table, inhaled, then exhaled like he was meditating. "All right. Have it your way. Your mother and I are trying to give you a future. You don't want it? Fine. Be ungrateful. Be a little prick."

He couldn't process the *otherwise* I was searching for. I wanted to shake him, tell him that I loved him but that I wanted more than his life, and if he truly loved me, he would understand. I wasn't asking for a handout, just support. I wanted them to hear me, actually hear me. That would have meant the world.

I cleared my throat and stood up from the couch. The woman on the TV was still going totally nuts over those boots. Which were hideous.

"I'm sorry," I said. "I really am. I don't know why or how, but I want something other than this. I don't want to live in this town. I don't want to work in an auto shop or at a gas station. And I'm not saying those are bad things. They're just not for me. And I know it's hard for you to understand that. But I wish, for my sake, you could at least try to. Because one day, not that long from now, I'm going to be gone. Maybe even far away. And I'd like to believe that, even if my parents don't understand me, they can at least be happy for me."

Mom and Dad were silent for a while. The clouds of their cigarette smoke formed a weird fog around them, thick as the fog in their minds. I stood there for what felt like forever, hoping in my heart for an *I love you* or even just an *okay*.

Instead, Dad tossed the phone to Mom.

"Order the damn boots." He stubbed out his cigarette in the ashtray on the table. "Move out of the way, JT, you're blocking the TV."

I didn't say another word. I just went to my room and slammed the door. I looked down at my computer and it was still opened to John Denton's bio. His face, with generations of hard work for kids like me, staring at me. I thought of Seth, beautiful Seth, and how much he believed in me. In that moment, I knew that no idea was too crazy. I had nothing to lose. Whatever it would take, I was getting out of Clearwater. As soon as possible. Once and for all. Give me a wig, I was going to win it—the scholarship, the title, everything. I was going to be THE Miss Drag Teen, and not just for Seth, not just for Heather or John Denton, but for me.

# chapter SIX

"I MIGHT REGRET THIS, BUT I want to do it."

I stood, trembling ever so slightly, on Seth's doorstep. His perfectly angular face immediately lit up like a Christmas tree.

"I've got to do something. I can't get stuck here. I can't work at a gas station for the rest of my life. Maybe they'll laugh and boo all over again, maybe I'll fall on my face and disgrace the entire legacy of John Denton, but I'm not in the position to turn down any opportunity. I just have to do it."

Seth grabbed my hands and pulled me into the foyer of his house. Seth's house was the kind of house that was always cozy and clean, with the walls covered by smiling family vacation photos from fancy exotic places like Charleston, South Carolina.

"This is wonderful. This is one of those moments where your life is on the verge of immense change, JT!"

Seth was being a bit overdramatic, but overdramatic or not, it felt really nice to see somebody excited for me. He bounced across the living room to his phone just as his mom walked in.

"We need to call Heather and tell her too," he said to me.

"Tell Heather what?" Seth's mom asked with her warm smile. Seth's mom was the kind of mom that you see on old sit-coms: pretty, sweet, slightly naive, and with a heart the size of Texas for her only son.

"About spring break."

"Oh! Are you boys going down to Daytona with the kids from school?" Seth's mom seemed genuinely excited for us to be planning something fun.

"We sure are!"

"Huh?" I wondered aloud. Seth squeezed my hand, shutting me up.

"Can we borrow your car?" he asked.

Seth's mom didn't even stop to think about it; she just maintained the same sweet mom smile she always had. This was either because she was genuinely a good-hearted person or because she had more Botox pumped in her face than the entire audience at the Golden Globes. Seth's dad was a local plastic surgeon and Seth's mom was his eerie masterpiece.

"Of course!" she chirped. "You guys hungry? I'm making guacamole!"

She went back to the kitchen, humming some kind of old jazz song under her breath. It was hard not to envy Seth's family. Their nice house, his always-perky mom, his wealthy dad who actually believed in college being something that wasn't just for, as my dad always called them, "snooty glasses-wearing types."

"What are you talking about?!" I whispered to Seth once his mom was out of earshot.

"My parents have been hounding me about going to spring break in Daytona with the rest of the school. They're all about the 'full high school experience.' Which, if you grow up in Florida, is supposed to mean beer bashes and wet T-shirt contests in Daytona. They told me they'd even pay for it. That'll cover our gas up to New York."

Seth picked up his phone and texted Heather the news, with the newly added detail of having a car, while I tried to process the fact that this was actually going to happen. I was going to New York for a competition that could possibly win me a full college scholarship. It all sounded too good to be true, and deep in my heart I knew it probably was.

Seth finished his text with a flourish of emojis, and spun around to kiss me.

"Now. We have got *a lot* of work to do!"


While Seth's parents were always encouraging Seth to have a good time, my parents were the complete opposite. Spring break was only a week away, and if I didn't turn in my application to do the pageant within the next twenty-four hours, I could kiss the whole opportunity good-bye.

I sat in my room, staring at the application form on the pageant website, listening to the ongoing drone of some detective TV show my parents were watching in the living room. Sometimes I wondered if the only reason people loved watching all those shows about horrible crimes is because it made them feel like slightly less terrible people.

I was scared to come right out and ask my parents for permission to go on the trip, even though the trip I was going to tell them about wasn't even the real trip itself. Daytona Beach was something my parents could understand. Daytona Beach was the kind of place people like my parents consider paradise. I was sure they'd gone there for *their* spring break. All I had to do was get them to say okay to that and then I'd have the entire week to myself to do the pageant, to breathe, to go nowhere near their dumpy gas station. But how could I even begin to ask them? Their inability to ever actually understand me made any conversation with them nearly impossible. It was as if they always knew exactly what I didn't want to hear, which meant that in the moments of attempting to stand up for myself, I felt so small. One *no* from them and I cowered down into the little-kid version of myself that had been so scared of ever crossing them.

The more time I spent thinking about the pageant, the more excited I allowed myself to get. Imagining myself in a great wig was about as exciting a thought as my mind could muster.

When I was little, before I saw *To Wong Foo*, I didn't know what a drag queen was, or what the term *drag* even meant . . . but I had this wig. It was slightly shorter than shoulder length, a brown, wavy wig my nana had worn during chemo. Nana had fought lung cancer for as long as I could remember, but she was stubborn as you could get, so she lived with it for way longer than they expected. Nana lived about twenty minutes away from us, and every couple weekends or so my parents would let me stay over with her for a few nights. She lived alone—my grandpa had died when I was a baby—and she liked having the company. Especially if the company was me.

I was her favorite, and she didn't mind telling anybody that, even her own son. She'd let me stay up way past my bedtime watching old movies, with fabulous songs, glamorous dresses, epic scenery. As we watched together she'd regale me with stories about the first time she'd seen each movie, and how she'd only paid a nickel to see it. Nana claimed so many things only cost a nickel *in my day* that I wondered how anyone had ever made any money at all.

She always let me sleep in her bed because my bedroom was in the back of the house, overlooking her big, dark, spooky backyard. An owl lived there, hooting and glaring with its glowing eyes every night, for as long as I could remember. It was terrifying the way it ominously glowed in the darkness. She always told me, though, that it was a good thing that the owl was watching over the two of us. Eventually I believed her. Nana had that kind of power about her; she made you believe in magic.

As the cancer got worse and the chemo more frequent, she always wore a turban to cover up her hair loss. It made her look like a really old genie. She also had a wig she'd purchased when she first started the chemo, but she didn't like wearing it because it was too itchy and, as she said, "I've got cancer, I'm not in a school play, for God's sake!"

I became obsessed with this wig. She kept it in a cabinet right by the vanity in her room, on one of those Styrofoam heads—

this one with a face hand-drawn by yours truly. Every time I'd go over to her house she'd let me take the wig out, brush it, and wear it. I loved the feeling of this gorgeous hair on my head. I loved looking at myself in the mirror as I was wearing it. I loved the feeling of looking like someone else.

Nana's cancer got real bad right around my eleventh birthday, and it became clearer and clearer to all of us, including to her, that she was going to die. We went over to her house one day and she had a birthday present wrapped up for me. My parents said something about how she shouldn't be buying me presents when she was so sick, and she told them to screw off. Inside the package was a Levi's denim jacket she must have ordered from a catalog. It was nice, and I was thankful, but it was nothing out of the ordinary. It wasn't until we were leaving that Nana whispered to me to look under the tissue paper inside the box. In the backseat of my parents' car, I looked—and there, underneath the tissue paper, was the wig and a note from Nana that said, *For when you're feeling blue.*

I kept the wig in that same box underneath my bed from that day on, and whenever I felt blue or nervous or mad or just needed a moment to smile, I'd pull out the box, put on the wig, look at myself in the mirror, and for the first time all day, I'd feel capable of anything. This was probably why I understood why the characters in *To Wong Foo* were doing what they were doing, because any time I put on that wig I felt like a star.

Maybe it was just something in my blood. Maybe it was Nana's spirit looking down on me and telling me I was going to be okay. Or maybe it was a combination. Either way, that afternoon, as I waited to tell my parents about spring break, I put it on. I looked at myself in the mirror and reminded myself that I had nothing to be afraid of. I'd always have Nana on my side. I could feel her cheering me on to take the first step toward my dreams.

"And I'm sure you both understand that spring break is a rite of passage for somebody my age, and you don't have to worry about it costing you money because Seth's offered to take care of it," I said, halfway through my plea to get the week off from the gas station.

My parents hadn't looked up from the TV once, except to tell me to move because I was blocking Mariska Hargitay.

"So . . . may I?"

"I don't care—ask your father," my mother said, focusing on the TV and not actually looking at my father, who was sitting directly next to her.

When the show went to a commercial, my father stood up and walked to the kitchen to get another beer. Then he cracked open the can as he walked back to his seat, as if he liked to leave me hanging.

Finally, he said, "If I say yes, you gotta work double time all next month."

My voice cracked with excitement as I promised that I'd work triple time if that's what it would take. They didn't put up too much of an argument—not because they cared but because the show was starting back and they wanted me to shut up. I ran back to my room, thanking the spirit of Nana. Then I lay down on my bed and texted Seth:

*New York, here we come.*

# chapter **seveN**

WITH THE ISSUE OF MY parents behind me and the first day of spring break being four nights away, I sent in my application for the pageant, which made the whole thing feel real, official, and utterly intimidating. The application itself was pretty minimal and standard; they wouldn't expect me to really explain myself until I was standing in front of hundreds of strangers onstage. The minute I sent it off and got the email confirmation that I was officially a contestant, I broke into a panic-fueled sweat. In the confirmation, they repeated the segment requirements: talent, interview, evening gown, and that incredibly intimidating speech about what drag means to you.

Public speaking aside (I'd passed out during my fifth-grade spelling bee on the word *altogether*, for goodness' sake!), the biggest problem with this speech would be the fact that I wasn't sure why I should be crowned the Drag Teen over anyone else. Sure, I needed the money—but that didn't mean I deserved it. Convincing a panel of judges you're worthy of first place is tough when you yourself think you're a loser.

I didn't tell Seth and Heather any of this. After agreeing to go, I tried to keep all my fears to myself. They were giving up their spring break to go on this adventure with me. All they should be getting back from me was gratitude, not angst.

Because he didn't have to worry about my mental health, Seth focused on other, more mundane road-trip matters.

"We'll definitely need a playlist," he said to me and Heather at lunch on the Friday before we were leaving. As he did, he marked the word *playlist* into the notebook where he was creating a list of things to bring with us on the road. "I should probably handle that since you both have bad taste in music."

"How dare you!" Heather said, slamming her miniature carton of fat-free milk onto her lunch tray and spilling a little white puddle onto her Salisbury steak. "I have great taste in music. I pride myself on having no understanding of Katy Perry whatsoever!"

"How about you both make playlists?" I interrupted. "We're driving from Florida to New York. Something tells me we'll have time for both."

"Now. I did the math and we're going to need roughly four hundred dollars in gas. I've got that covered—"

"No!" I protested. "That makes me feel bad. The only reason we're doing this is because of me. You shouldn't have to spend your own money to get me to New York to be in some dumb pageant."

Seth threw his hand in the air. "First of all, the pageant isn't dumb, and you really need to stop saying that or you're going to create that as the narrative in your head and not try hard enough." (Seth read WAY too much O magazine.) "Second of all, it's my parents' money. They have a lot of it, too much of it, and it's from cutting into people's faces in an attempt to make them look younger but ultimately just turning them into people who look like forgotten Muppets that got thrown out for being too strange-looking. So, if I'm not spending it on getting my boyfriend to a drag pageant and his future, then I don't know what I'm doing with my life."

Seth's adorable grin could have convinced me to do anything. But accepting his money was still hard, even if it was his parents' money. It was like he was Robin Hood, Heather was Maid Marian, and I was one of the beggar children they robbed the rich for.

But you can't expect Robin Hood to understand that even good deeds lead to a feeling of indebtedness. He continued to grin, saying, "So. We're doing this? Like, for real? This Sunday, we're going to drive to New York City?"

He looked across the table at me. I looked at Heather. Heather looked back to Seth. As if on cue, slowly, we all nodded yes.


Two days later, Seth's car was packed to the brim with luggage. We carefully avoided his mom's curiosity about why we'd need so much stuff in Daytona Beach by blaming Heather's indecisiveness about what to wear. Seth's mom had every right to raise an eyebrow, but the bottom line was that because of all her plastic surgery, she literally couldn't.

We'd *all* way overpacked, but that was the thing about drag—it wasn't about to allow us to travel lightly. I had two suitcases of clothes I'd borrowed from Heather, the wig from Nana, every pair of heels I could squeeze my feet into from the local thrift shop, and a major suitcase for my makeup. I had packed so much stuff for drag that I'd barely had enough room for my civilian clothes.

I called shotgun and Heather took the backseat. The agreement was that we'd drive in shifts—or rather that Seth and I would drive in shifts, while Heather would rest in the backseat. Heather was fine if she was just driving around Florida, but interstate freeways were a different matter altogether. Heather had failed her driver's test four times and the only reason she'd passed it the fifth time was because the lady at the DMV was tired of having to talk to her.

We were breaking up the trip over the course of three days because that's what we'd seen people do on road trips in movies. We'd drive until we got too tired, we'd stay at a motel near the interstate, then we'd get up the next morning to do it again. Our goal for the first day was to get to South Carolina before dark.

We hit the road, Seth's mix of pop music as our soundtrack as we pulled onto the interstate, leaving Clearwater behind us. I could barely believe it was really happening.

We passed the time with car trip games; we played Résumé, which was a game I claimed to have made up but that I'm sure I didn't. You named an actress and every time it was your turn you had to name one of that actress's movies. The game lasted until no one could name another movie. I was essentially unstoppable at this game because I had seen pretty much every movie any famous actress had ever made. It didn't occur to me until I had beaten everyone through Sandra Bullock, Reese Witherspoon, Meryl Streep, and Jennifer Lawrence that none of us had ever, ever considered playing the game with a man's name.

"Why would we do that?" Heather scoffed at my question, and she had a valid point. One of the uniting bonds between Heather and me was that we refused to see movies without a strong female lead. Heather argued it was our feminism, but in reality I think it was just that Nana had instilled me with good taste when it came to movies.

It was beginning to get dark out, the sun setting behind a McDonald's golden arches. We'd been driving for a while, maybe seven hours, long enough that we'd listened to "Firework" thirty-three times and Heather had told us the story about the time her parents left her at the grocery store, twice. A sign advertised forty-dollar rooms three miles ahead, and we decided we'd gotten far enough for one day. Plus, forty dollars was our exact budget for a room that night, so we pulled off onto the exit and into the parking lot for the Bel Air Inn.

Seth checked us in while Heather and I waited in the car. We figured a group of three teenagers paying for one room in cash might look a bit suspect. Our plan was that Seth would break down crying and tell them he was in town for a funeral if they asked why a seventeen-year-old was traveling alone. They didn't, though—the Bel Air Inn didn't seem like the kind of place where people paid a lot of attention to who was coming or going. The two-floor building looked like something out of a horror movie, surrounding a pool that was a color I'd never seen before—not blue, not green, not yellow, but something in between all three. There was nothing else within eyeshot except for a diner and a gas station; only a few cars and Mack trucks were parked in the motel parking lot, and the snack machine outside our first-floor room was out of everything but gum that looked like it had been in there since before I was born.

Our room was even rougher than the rest of the place. The two double beds advertised ended up being one double bed and the headboard of a second one. Which left us to speculate where the other mattress and bed frame had gone and why anyone would have wanted them.

"Bedbug farmer?" Heather guessed.

"Maybe they put it into the Smithsonian as part of an exhibit on crime scenes," Seth theorized.

"Maybe it just went for a walk," I reasoned. "I mean, if you were a bed, would you want to stay here?"

"Well, until it comes back, we have a problem. We can't all fit in a double bed," Heather complained. "Call the front desk and ask for a rollaway or something."

Seth shook his head. "We can't. I told them it was just me, remember? They'll probably charge more if I ask." Riskily, he plopped his suitcase onto the filthy carpet.

"Just to play devil's advocate," I argued, "I don't think this is the kind of place that will ask that many questions. It feels like the kind of place you could kill someone and housekeeping would simply vacuum around the body. Or incorporate it into the decor. That lamp looks like a salesman after his third coronary, no?"

"Do *you* want to be the one to talk to the guy behind the front desk?" Seth challenged. "I think his name was Snarly Deathbringer. Any takers?"

Heather and I decided it was best to just suck it up and share the bed with one another both out of fear but mainly because of general teenage laziness. It would be a tight squeeze, but it was just the one night. Besides, something told me we didn't want to see what was rolled away inside a rollaway bed at this place.

"What are we going to do with our night?" Heather dug a sweater out of her suitcase, since the AC in the room was on some kind of arctic setting and the on/off switch must have joined the missing bed on its moonlit stroll.

"Um. Sleep, right?" I asked. "Isn't that the point?"

"No, Heather's right. We should do something! This is the first night of our adventure. Let's explore!" Seth was way too energetic for someone who had just spent seven hours in a car. They both were, actually. Then again, I wasn't exactly in a hurry to squeeze into the double bed with the two of them either.

"Where exactly do you plan to explore?" I pointed out the window at the barren fields and interstate outside. "That diner? Or the gas station? How can you choose between such scintillating options?"

Heather and Seth, ready for adventure, ignored my sarcasm. Heather tossed the car keys to Seth.

"You're right. We ought to eat first."

*　*　*

The diner across the street was almost as disgusting as our motel room, but only almost. It was set up like your typical diner, with a long counter going through the center of the room and a few tables in the corner. Someone must have put in at least twenty dollars' worth of quarters before we got there because the jukebox never stopped playing Christian rock music. We sat down at a table near the front, my hands sticking to the table the minute I touched it.

"You guys, why do I feel like everybody is staring at us?" Heather asked, surveying the room. I turned and saw that her feeling was correct: Every single eye in the place was focused on us.

"I suppose they've never seen a guy on the verge of being crowned Miss Drag Teen before," Seth said, waving his hand in dismissal and peeling the menu off the linoleum tabletop. "Now. Do you think this place has any vegan options?"

We were all so far from vegan that we'd had KFC for lunch earlier, but we always liked to joke about snobby city-people things like that. One time we'd dared Heather to ask Mrs. Irene, our school lunch lady, for something gluten-free, and Mrs. Irene had almost thrown a chicken-fried steak at her. Joking about things like that was our way of feeling a little bit closer to life in a big city where people would get us.

"Ready?" a very old waitress with a name tag specifying her as Sheila asked. She didn't betray even a trace of a smile.

We were caught off guard and all ordered burgers just because it would get her away from our table quicker.

"She seems fun." Heather rolled her eyes.

"Okay, so, JT," Seth said, ripping a page from his ever-present notebook. "I think you should write out a to-do list of what needs to be done before the pageant. We need to be prepared by the time we get to New York."

"That's a great idea." Heather drummed her hands on the table excitedly. "I love lists."

"What kind of list?" I asked.

"Well, for one, the four key words from John Denton. That's ultimately what this whole competition is about, right?" Seth pulled the pageant website up on his phone.

"And what are they again?"

Seth cleared his throat. "Glamour. Talent. Heart. And soul."

When I didn't make a move for the pen, he wrote down the four intimidating words on a napkin.

"What does that even mean?" I asked. "How do you find soul—I mean, besides listening to Mary J. Blige circa twenty years ago?"

"They mean it in a more general, emotional sense," Seth clarified. "What makes up your soul?"

Sheila, the waitress, sat our drinks down on the table and shot Seth a strange look as she heard the tail end of his statement.

"I have absolutely no idea what that means," I said.

Heather was busily staring across the room. "Um. The guy in the corner totally just waved at me. Don't look." As if on cue, both Seth and I turned around and looked. "You guys!"

The guy in the window was pretty cute. Hipster cute, no less. Tattoos, shaggy hair, most likely a little smelly on purpose. He was exactly Heather's type.

"How old is he, you think?" she asked.

Seth looked over. "Probably our age, or one of those people with that disease that makes you age really slowly and he's, like, fifty-four. Go say hello."

Heather nearly spat her water. "What the hell is your problem? Why do you keep trying to get me to talk to people any time we go out to eat?"

She had a point. I remembered last time all too well.

"Come on, Seth," I said. "This is a diner. People don't go over and say hello in diners."

"Why not? Look. We're on an adventure. You are going to do drag again, JT. We're all seeing New York for the first time ever while lying to our families. Clearly we all owe it to ourselves to make this adventure special. No, people don't walk over and say hello in diners, but they do in adventures, and like I told you the other day . . . you two need a dose of confidence and I refuse to hear any more about it. Go."

Seth spoke with such purpose that Heather, instead of arguing, got up and walked over to the guy's table.

"I can't believe you got her to do that again," I whispered as we pretended not to watch. From the animation of the guy's body language and the smile on Heather's face, it looked as though it was going well this time.

"Hey. I have a question," I asked with some trepidation.

"The other night, you know how you said you might go to Ithaca or whatever?"

"Uh-huh."

"Well, Heather said nobody ever ends up with—"

Heather rushed back over with a big grin.

"Well?!" Seth whispered really loudly as she sat back down.

"Well. Get this. He's straight."

"That's a good first step," Seth quipped.

"And the friend he's with is gay—"

Both Seth and I flipped our heads back around to get a better look at the alleged gay friend. He was a few years older than the straight guy, maybe early twenties.

"And get this. They're on their way to a gay bar that's nearby. They said it's only, like, a fifteen-minute drive. You guys in?"

A gay bar? None of us had ever been in a gay bar before. We'd all imagined what they were like, how magical they would prove to be, the kind of places where we'd walk in and immediately fit in. However, we were seventeen—no decent establishment would allow three teenagers to simply walk in on a Saturday night.

"Apparently, this place *never* checks IDs," Heather went on, clearing up my questions of whether or not this was a decent establishment.

"YES!" Seth shouted, so loud most people in the diner heard him. "Come on, JT. It'll be fun!"

I was often in this position, the one who needed to be coerced into having fun. I was sick of it. I didn't want to keep being that guy. Seth didn't like that guy. I needed to follow his lead—this was an adventure, and adventures meant stepping out of your box. Sure, I'd already done so by leaving Clearwater, but if I expected not to lose my mind once hitting New York, it was high time I started jumping out of my comfort zone.

A gay bar in the middle of South Carolina seemed like a good enough place to start.

# chapter **EIGHT**

WE FOLLOWED OUR NEW FRIENDS from the diner in
Seth's car. I was willing to go outside my box as far as the gay
bar was concerned, but I wasn't going to step as far as getting in
a car with strangers. The gay bar, Sugarbaker's, was more than
twenty minutes away, and when we pulled up to the place I was
sure we had the wrong address. It was in a small strip mall,
sandwiched between a Starbucks and a pet store. The guys
from the diner, whose names I still hadn't learned, were right
about IDs not being needed at the door. I wasn't interested in
drinking—as usual, the idea grossed me out—so I was happy to
be the designated driver.

Even though it was a run-down pit of a bar, it was our first
gay bar, and it immediately felt sorta magical, as much as a
place that smelled like bleach and stale beer could. It wasn't
really the place itself but the atmosphere, the little universe
housed within its four walls. Outside was a small southern
Podunk town with a Bible bookstore connected to an Arby's,
but inside there was a cool little oasis for gay people from all
walks of life, to come inside and breathe easy, even just for the

night. It looked like a lot of gay bars I'd seen in movies, but smaller, and with fewer glow sticks. A dusty disco ball hung in the center of the room, bathing everything in little white specks. Beer signs made the walls glow, and a few clusters of people were scattered around the bar. This was a Sunday night and I'd venture to guess the place was less than half full. Some old disco song was playing, way too loudly, as I followed Seth and Heather inside to meet our new friends at the bar.

"Hi!" Heather called out to the guys over the music. They introduced themselves back: Alex, the gay one, was the type of guy whose perfect body was likely documented in a plethora of Instagram shirtless selfies, crowned by one of those confident pearly white smiles that make you either a movie star or cult leader, or both. Matt, the straight, cute hipster guy, must have been around our age. From the get-go, he smiled flirtatiously at Heather. I could see her blush and try to cover it up; it was sweet to see Heather like that. Romance avoided Heather almost as much as I avoided going to doll conventions with my mother.

"Guys, this is JT and Seth," Heather, our go-between, said. Both Matt and Alex shook our hands.

Seth leaned forward and whispered to them, "None of us have ever been in a gay bar before!"

The guys laughed and asked what we wanted to drink. I asked for a Diet Coke while Heather and Seth shrugged.

"I'll get you two vodka cranberries." Alex pulled a shiny American Express card out of his wallet. "They're disgusting but they're part of the gay bar experience."

At first I thought the bartender was catching onto Seth being underage, but then I realized he was just checking him out. In fact, every guy in the bar was checking Seth out. The only people who seemed to be immune were the cluster of lesbians playing pool. This wasn't all that strange—people always noticed Seth's beauty. But I'd never been in a room where every single guy was staring at him at once. The bartender handed him his drink and, with a wink, told him it was on the house. I could feel my skin crawl.

We made our way to a little booth in the corner. Heather was already talking Matt's ear off, while Alex had cornered Seth, grilling him about his life.

"You sure do!" I awkwardly chimed in after Seth's story about his love of the beach. I just wanted to feel included in the conversation, but it was evident that Alex couldn't have cared less about what I had to say.

How could I be in a gay bar for the first time ever, finally, and still feel like an outsider? Wasn't the whole point of going to a gay bar to feel not left out? No one was noticing me or giving me strange looks, which made it even worse; they only stared at Seth and Alex, and a handful of the other cute guys in the room. I started to wonder if people thought Alex and Seth were a couple. After all, they looked good together, like the kind of couple you'd see in a movie where people end up kissing in the rain and a dog somehow survives an epic catastrophe. I'd always known I was a weird match for Seth; if he was a ten, I was more of a two, a three *maybe* if I was wearing my cute hoodie. Seeing a guy as hot as Alex blatantly flirting with him made me feel about as sure of this insecurity as I'd ever felt.

"So, we have to be in New York by Wednesday." Seth was midway into explaining the reason for our trip as he patted my knee. Heather and Matt had moved to the dance floor. "Come next weekend, JT here is going to be crowned America's number-one drag teen."

"So you're a drag queen?" Alex asked, with a slight but very apparent tone of judgment. I could feel my cheeks getting redder by the second.

"Well, sorta," I sputtered. "I mean, I've only done it once before, but they convinced me to try again because there's a scholarship. I don't know what I was thinking. I'm not very good at it."

"He's underplaying it," Seth butted in. "The one time he did it, he actually sang, and he was breathtaking."

"Yeah, so breathtaking that everyone in the room laughed at me and booed."

I could tell Seth was getting agitated; nothing bothered him more than when I talked badly about myself, especially in front of strangers. It was his way of showing support, of course, but ultimately it was just really annoying.

"That's only because you didn't know how to do all the makeup and costuming routines. Which I've told you we're going to figure out before we get to New York. There are YouTube tutorials for that." Seth looked back at Alex with a guilty grin. "Let's just say, neither JT nor I understood the importance of tucking."

Alex wasn't paying a bit of attention; he was too busy looking Seth up and down, like he was shopping for a new sofa.

"Do you swim? You look like you probably swim," Alex asked.

"Not really. I run track, though." Seth shrugged, seeming not to pick up on how longingly Alex was looking at him.

"Hm. Yeah. I see that."

I tried not to get jealous because Seth hated it when I did, but it was getting a little difficult to pretend I wasn't noticing the way this guy was smiling at my boyfriend. Plus, even I knew that *swimmer* was a gay code word for *hot body*. Had he learned how to flirt from some sort of advice book, *How to Be a Douchebag in One Easy Step*? I took a deep breath to calm down.

"Hey." Alex flicked his pretty brown hair over his ear as he glanced over at me. "Sorry, man. What was your name again?"

"JT."

"Right. See her over there?" He pointed at an old drag queen in the corner of the room who was setting up a microphone on a little stage. "That's Bambi. She's been around forever. She's drag royalty around here. If you give her twenty bucks, she'd probably teach you everything you need to know. To be honest, for twenty bucks I'm pretty sure Bambi would do anything you asked her to do."

Bambi looked a lot older than my parents; she wasn't fat, but she was nowhere near thin. She wore an unflattering hot-pink pantsuit with a blond wig that was so much bigger than her head that I genuinely wondered how she was able to keep it up there, gravity being what it is. One thing was clear, though— she knew drag inside and out, and it showed. Her makeup was flawless, the contouring and shading giving her face a striking movie-star look. Plus, she maneuvered on heels like they were a pair of Crocs.

"Oh, I don't want to bother her," I said. "It looks like she's getting ready to do a show or something."

I've always sucked at talking to strangers, especially when they're in fifty-pound blond wigs.

"Oh, don't be silly, JT!" Seth started pushing me over to her. "You should talk to her about the pageant. Ask her about how to do the makeup shading and stuff. Look at her—she clearly knows what she's doing. Seriously, go over there!"

Now I was embarrassed, since I was beginning to look like a clingy weirdo in front of this Alex guy if I didn't go over there. Besides, I wasn't sure how much longer I could listen to him ask my boyfriend about his athletic prowess anyway, so I awkwardly wandered over.

Bambi was focused on the sound equipment and I was immediately impressed to notice she could do all this manual labor in press-on pink nails. As I walked over, she glanced up at me.

"Sorry. Karaoke doesn't start for another thirty minutes, hon."

"Oh. No. I just wanted to say hi. I'm sorry, you're busy." I began stuttering. "I-I'll leave you alone."

"Darling, I'm a forty-year-old drag queen in the dregs of South Carolina—how busy do you actually think I am?" she asked, throwing me quite a curveball with the "forty-year-old" part. The last time Bambi would have passed for forty very well might have been forty years ago.

"Um. Alex, that guy over there, said you might show me how to do proper drag makeup if I give you twenty bucks." I began vomiting up my life story. "We're visiting from Florida. See, I'm driving up to New York for this pageant . . . it's a drag pageant, for teens, the Miss Drag Teen Pageant. He said I should talk to you because you're drag royalty. Last time I tried drag, I was so excited, but then it went really badly. I didn't know how to do the makeup and my wig sucked and I—"

Bambi held up her hand for me to stop.

"If I show you what to do, will you shut up?"

I motioned zipping my lips, which when you really think about it would be horrific and unforgettably painful.

"Fine. Follow me."

She parted the curtain behind the makeshift stage and I followed her into the tiny backstage area. The room was clearly meant to be a janitor's closet, but Bambi had turned it into a star dressing room, or as close to a star dressing room as a janitor's closet could get. The walls were covered in old glamour shots of actresses, models, and a much younger-looking Bambi. A small vanity was wedged in the corner, the counter of which was covered in makeup pencils, brushes, sponges, and endless rows of fake eyelashes. Towering over us were three shelves filled with wigs in a rainbow of colors on Styrofoam heads. The whole place smelled like hair spray, cigarettes, bleach, and showbiz. I was home.

Bambi turned the knob on a box of wine wedged between two impressively tall go-go boots, filling a coffee cup to the brim.

"Want a drink?" she offered.

"I'm seventeen."

"And your point is?"

"Naw, I don't drink."

She squinted her eyes at me and shook her head. "Kids these days. Sit down."

She directed me to the little stool in front of the vanity. As I sat down, she clicked on the little lightbulbs surrounding the mirror, nearly blinding me. Then she leaned down to stretch a wig cap onto my head.

"You've got a nice shape to your face, so that's a good first step."

"Thanks."

She held her palm in front of my eyebrows and looked at me from varying angles, like an artist surveying her blank canvas. She muttered something to herself, then picked up a tube of white makeup and a brush. She began to paint the white over my eyebrows, making them slowly disappear like grass under snow. I've always had thick eyebrows, and the last time I'd tried to do my own makeup, I just left them there, which made me look like a very pretty garden gnome.

"See what I'm doing here, darling? In order to create a face, you've got to start over entirely, and the first thing to go should always be the eyebrows. Some queens pluck theirs, but that crap looks just too damn weird for me in the daylight, so I cover mine up. I'm old school like that."

She began covering my face with a really pale foundation, turning the entire thing into one shade, on which she began using a darker color to make me look like I had cheekbones.

"*Shading* and *contouring* are your new favorite words. They're the most important part of conquering your face."

The dark lines and shadows were transforming my face into something entirely unrecognizable. Something glamorous.

"Drag is armor, darling. No matter how you look at it. Once I become Bambi, nobody can hurt me. Not my family, not the drunk assholes at the bar, nobody. A good lace-front wig and the right contouring are as strong a bulletproof vest as I've ever needed."

I'd never thought about that before, but it made sense. I had always felt more beautiful when I put on a wig and sang a song from *Wicked* in my bedroom than I did in regular everyday life.

"I never liked myself, darling. Ever. Always felt like the outsider, but you know what? It took me until I was already middle-aged to build the courage to do it, but the minute I put on a wig and dress and got onstage for the first time? I felt like I could be president of the United States if I wanted to be."

"But when you're not in drag, when you go back to just being everyday you, does it all go away?" I had to ask. "The good feelings you have about yourself?"

She had moved on to putting on my eye shadow, a greenish blue that made my eyes look less gray than normal.

"Maybe it did a long time ago. But now? Going up onstage in front of people, dressed like this, feeling this fabulous? I've fallen madly in love with myself, and nowadays I feel just as in love with myself out of my wig as I do in it. But I also know that I'll make better tips if I'm in it."

It was quiet for a while as she began covering the extreme contouring shapes with powder. I tried not to sneeze.

"Hey, how do you come up with a name? A drag name, I mean."

"Every queen has her own theory. First pet's name, street you grew up on, or some crap like that. All that's silly, if you ask me. When you're ready for your drag name, it just plain finds you." She showed me the foundation she was using and told me how much was too much, muttering something about how some queens turn out looking like they just came from Sherwin-Williams.

"What about yours?" I asked. "What does Bambi mean?"

She laughed. "It's stupid. Bambi is short for Bambi's Mother. You know, like the cartoon? That bitch was a survivor. I mean, she died in the end, but damn, she put up a fight to stick around as long as she did. I guess I saw a lot of myself in her, and one day it just hit me."

"Do you have any ideas for mine?"

Bambi stepped away from the chair and looked at me sternly. "I'm not your fairy godmother, darling. Like I said, when the time is right, it'll find *you*." She sounded a lot more like a fairy godmother than she had probably intended.

"So." She picked up her cup, taking a large gulp. "That pretty-looking boy I saw you sitting with out there? Is he your boyfriend or what?"

"Uh-huh, he is."

"So what do you have to feel bad about? You're young, you've got a cute boyfriend, and by the time I'm finished, you're going to look marvelous."

"Well, you saw him."

Bambi began drawing on my new thin eyebrows. "I did. And your point is?"

"Well, he's really hot. Like epically hot. Everyone in the bar stared at him when he came in. I feel like it's only a matter of time before he wakes up and realizes he could do way better than me. My friend says nobody ends up with his or her first boyfriend, and she's probably right. Right?"

Bambi looked at me through the mirror. "Self-pity is an ugly color on you, darling. It's an ugly color on all of us, except maybe Joni Mitchell. Tilt your head back, look at the ceiling, and don't blink." She began tracing my eyelids with the pencil. Not blinking was proving to be quite a challenge. "Until I met my husband five years ago, I'd been single since, well, most of my life. And I used to blame it on this or that, but it wasn't until I started performing in drag and letting myself feel as free as I feel now that I realized why."

"Why?" I asked, accidentally blinking. "Sorry!"

"It's like RuPaul says: If you can't love yourself, how in the hell are you going to love somebody else?"

She finished with the eyeliner and moved on to fake eyelashes, meticulously dabbing on small strips of glue.

"I know what it's like to be a seventeen-year-old gay boy who can only feel confident in a pair of heels, darling, but all that talk from those famous gay people saying it gets better is horseshit unless you put in the effort. Understand?"

"Yes, but—"

"Close your lips and keep them closed so I can finish my wise old fabulous queen speech, and also so I can put your lipstick on. Everything is temporary, darling—the bad stuff, sure, but the good stuff too, and you won't come close to really living and enjoying what you've got in front of you until you accept that annoying little truth. Life is short. Don't be like I was. Don't take until you're middle-aged to enjoy it. You're seventeen—make mistakes, get your heart broken, get booed at, humiliate yourself, get jealous of guys you think are more hand-some than you flirting with your boyfriend in bars . . . but remember that even your worst feeling, or meanest thought about yourself? It's all temporary, so just enjoy it."

"But the good stuff is too?"

"Yep. And sometimes? That's going to really suck."

We were both quiet suddenly. The room was too, as it went from one song to another in the bar outside. The short gap of silence felt like forever. Within it, Bambi placed a bright green, curled, cropped-at-the-shoulders wig on my head.

"Look," she said, with the flourish of a magician completing a trick.

I saw myself in the mirror and gasped. I looked like a real, honest to God, legit drag queen. Not just some boy in a dress.

"I look . . ." But I couldn't finish the sentence, not in that moment. Words failed me.

"*Stunning*, darling."

"Can I take a selfie with you?"

Bambi rolled her eyes as she began to put her makeup tools back where they came from. "You kids reach for a camera the minute anything feels even the slightest bit okay, don't you?"

she said as leaned in beside me and immediately struck the kind of pose that told me she was no stranger to taking a selfie.

"Perfect," I said.

I dug into my pocket and felt the list of John Denton To-Dos. Seth had handed it over to me when we left. There at the top of the list was glamour. I picked up a makeup pencil.

"What's that you're doing?" Bambi asked.

"It's silly, but for this pageant they say the four keys are glamour, talent, heart, and soul."

"Well, if that face of yours isn't glamour, then I don't know what else is. However, if you're thinking of using one of my makeup pencils to write, you better think again." She yanked the pencil out of my hand and replaced it with a pen. I crossed off the word *glamour*. "Now, go out there and show that boy just how beautiful you look. You don't owe me twenty bucks—just be sure to thank me when you win that prize."

I got up and walked over to the curtain. But before I walked out, I turned back to Bambi. She was putting away her makeup brushes and pencils.

"Hey, Bambi?"

She looked over her shoulder. With her enormous wig and bright makeup, she looked like a drag queen chief, a respected elder of some long-lost tribe. And I guess in a lot of ways that's exactly what she was.

"Thanks," I said.

I walked back out through the little curtain, reentering the bar. I was so excited for Seth to see me, to see how great I looked, to see that despite all my whining, I really could do this after all. I could be a real drag queen. That's when I saw him dancing, slowly, to some crappy pop song, with Alex. I thought I might puke.

He immediately spotted me and stepped away from Alex, pointing at my makeover with a giant smile. I still felt humiliated, standing there in full drag from the neck up only. I didn't know what to do, so I ripped off the wig, threw it on the stage, and ran out the front door.

# chapter **NINE**

SETH WAS RIGHT BEHIND ME.

"JT! Wait!"

The parking lot was dark and mostly empty, the old sign written in a rainbow of neon colors, lighting our faces in reds and greens and blues as I snapped around to face him.

"What?" I asked. "What do you want?!"

I had already started crying, the tears mixing into the eyelash glue, creating a thick, tar-like sludge under my eyes.

"Listen to me. That wasn't what it looked like. We were all dancing to a fast song, but then it turned slow and Alex grabbed me and tried to dance, but I was pulling away right when you came out."

Seth reached for my hand but I wouldn't let him have it. I could now feel mascara running down my cheeks, but I was too upset to care enough to wipe it off.

He went on. "I know. He was being very flirty, but I told him I was with you and then we went to dance with Heather and Mark, but then Heather ran off—"

"She ran off? What do you mean?"

"Out of nowhere, she just insisted on taking a cab back to the motel," Seth said with a shrug.

"And you let her go off all by herself in the middle of some town we've never been to in our lives? Are you an idiot?"

Seth was clearly taken aback. "Hey, now, wait. I—"

"Why would you let her do something like that? So you could flirt with that guy in privacy while I was off with the drag queen? Is that it?" I fished Seth's keys out of my sweatshirt pocket. "Come on, we need to go right now and make sure she's okay."

"She's fine, JT. I wouldn't have put her in danger, you know that. She's not a baby, she—"

I wasn't listening. With two fake eyelashes slowly dripping down my cheek, I stomped my way across the gravel to our car.

"You can either come with me or stay here," I told him.

I got in the car and Seth rushed over to join me. As we started back to the motel, he attempted to further explain what had happened with Alex. I cut him off. I wasn't in the mood to hear it.

When we got back to the motel room, Heather was already fast asleep—snoring, in fact. All I wanted was to go to sleep and for the night to be over. I went into the bathroom and washed the rest of the makeup off my face—at this point, the once-glamorous face Bambi had created on me looked more like a piece of modern art someone would pay way too much money for, just to have the privilege of pretending to understand it.

Seth tapped on the door.

"Come in," I said.

He walked in behind me, already changed into his pajamas. I attempted to avoid eye contact.

"JT, I want you to let me explain what happened—"

"Not right now, okay? Not tonight."

Seth sighed and said fine. Then he brushed his teeth beside me, in silence.

"He was really, really handsome," I said, softly, as if saying it too loud would hurt more.

"And so are you, JT."

"Yeah, but not like him. Not like you. Not like some of those other guys at the bar. It made me feel like it's only a matter of time before you realize how much better you could do than me. Then you'll be gone and with someone as perfect as you."

Seth spat out his toothpaste and took my hands, his breath so minty.

"I am *not* perfect," he tried to assure me.

"But you are! You're in amazing shape, you're pretty, you're funny, you're smart, you're—"

"Stop it. I try so hard to make you realize how special you are, but it's like there's no point because you're never going to believe me."

"Do you think everything is temporary?" I asked. "Like, even the stuff that makes you happy?"

I could feel that tremble in the back of my throat that you get when you say something that scares you.

"Um, that's a pretty deep conversation for this late . . . but sure, yeah. Of course I do. Why?"

"So, this? Us? You think of this as just some temporary moment in our lives that's bound to end?"

"Babe, I was literally just dancing with him. I told you, we were all dancing to a fast song and it had just happened to switch to something slow when you walked out. It really meant nothing. You know that I love you."

I squeezed his hand and pulled him slightly closer. "No, but do you think of us as just some temporary thing? I mean, we're seventeen, right? Sometimes I wish I liked you less, or that I'd met you when I was older, or—"

"JT. I think of us and smile, I think of us and get so happy that I get to know what love feels like at our age."

"But do you think it's just temporary?"

"I think that everything is, yes."

"But doesn't that scare you? I mean, doesn't that make you feel like, what's the point?"

"No. It doesn't. It makes me less afraid. It makes me not worry. It makes me excited to live in the moment."

I wanted to feel that kind of excitement, that kind of freedom from inhibition. I wasn't sure if I'd ever genuinely felt "in the moment" in my life. If I were able to live in the moment, I probably would see exactly what he meant, that he really did love me. I would actually be able to hear the sweet words coming out of his mouth. (He *was* driving me across the country to a drag pageant, for God's sake.) I would probably see that Bambi was right about not overthinking so much. I leaned forward and kissed him, trying not to think of the future, of what I wanted our lives to someday be, of all my stupid plans, of every second-guessing thought I had happening in my head at every second of every day.

"JT, you're going to find what it is that puts you here, that makes you present, and you'll know when it happens, because you'll look around and realize that everything is okay. I promise."

I nodded, but inside my head, I wondered if I ever would.

# chapter TeN

WE GOT UP LATE THE next day and hit the road. I was thinking a lot about what Seth had said about finding my anchor into the moment. *How do I find that?* I wondered. *Or do I just wake up one day and have it? Like a zit?*

"Should we sing?" Seth's voice pierced the conversational silence of the car.

Heather didn't answer. In fact, she'd been quiet the entire morning, a very rare occurrence for her. I could see her in the rearview mirror sitting in the backseat, arms crossed. Despite her sunglasses covering her eyes, I could tell they were rolling. Seth and I hadn't asked her about what happened last night—we figured she'd tell us when she was ready.

"Or play one of those road-trip car games," Seth pressed on. "Do you guys know any?"

Heather remained silent.

"I'm not really awake enough for games," I said, staring out the window as an enormous billboard for a place that advertised HOT BABES AND WINGS went by. I couldn't imagine eating wings in front of anyone, let alone strippers.

"Okay, well, we need gas. I'm going to pull off."

Seth took the next exit, which was a barren wasteland somewhere in North Carolina, with only a gas station and a pizza place connected to a store called Baby Jesus's Books and Gifts in sight. At the station, Seth pumped the gas while Heather and I went inside for sodas. It was always weird for me to be in a gas station that wasn't the one I grew up in; a small part of me worried that the person behind the cash register would spot me, take off, and leave me to run the place the way my parents always had.

Quickly, I grabbed two Cokes for Seth and me.

"Want one?" I asked Heather.

She turned from a rack of healthy-looking snacks: dried fruit, nuts, and other stuff she never ate.

"Make mine diet," she said.

I grabbed a Diet Coke and gave her a look she would understand, a look that asked, *Since when do you eat or drink* anything *diet, you crazy person?*

"What?" she said defensively. "Those regular ones have a crazy number of calories. And the sugar? It's like drinking a cake."

I raised my eyebrows. I didn't think Heather had ever said the word *calorie* before in her life. That was one of the things I loved about her, that she was just as reckless with food as I was. A great night for Heather and me usually consisted of watching bad reality shows and eating as many snacks as we could until we fell asleep or ran out. She was like my sister in carbohydrates.

"Everything okay?" I asked.

"Yes. Why wouldn't everything be okay? Why can't I just be in a bad mood sometimes and not have something be wrong? Sometimes people just don't feel great, JT. There is nothing wrong with that."

She took the Diet Coke and huffed and puffed her way to the counter, picking up a bag of unsalted almonds on the way. Then, before reaching the counter, frustrated, she tossed the almonds onto a shelf and went for a bag of M&M'S instead. I hadn't seen Heather this upset since the third time KFC discontinued popcorn chicken.

Once we stepped outside, I squeezed her hand. The time had clearly come to talk about the previous night.

"Hey. You ran away from the bar last night. You've been weird and quiet all morning. Clearly something is wrong, and we might as well stop pretending it isn't, because we're way too close for that. So, what's up?"

She tried to yank away but I tightened my grip. She sighed, her eyes staring at a crack in the pavement.

"I'm fat, JT."

This wasn't news to me and it wasn't news to her.

"Hey, you're just—"

"No. Don't. You know I'm fat. I know I'm fat. And that cute guy who flirted with me last night? He knew I was fat too."

Her cheeks were getting flushed, like she might cry.

"What are you talking about?"

"That guy? Mark? The one I danced with at the bar? At the end of one of the slow dances, he kissed me. I told him he was handsome and you know what he told me?"

"What?"

"He said that I'd caught his attention because he'd never been with a fat girl before and he wanted to try something crazy."

Now tears were forming in her eyes. People coming in and out of the gas station stared as they passed us.

"It wasn't like he was even being mean about it. He was just being honest. He was just explaining to me that he'd only been with 'normal' girls. Like I'm some sort of freak. It's Seth's fault for making me talk to him. I need to stop listening to him. Having confidence is a load of BS. All it does is give you enough courage to go out and humiliate yourself."

I didn't know what to say that could comfort her because I didn't know if I actually disagreed with what she was saying. Seth didn't have to work to be confident because there was no reason he wouldn't be confident already. People like Heather and me, we didn't blend the way someone like Seth did, and I guess that was the whole secret to being confident: the ability to blend.

"Heather, you're beautiful." I attempted to sound assured. "You know that you're beautiful."

"How am I supposed to believe that? Coming from you? Look at how you see yourself, JT. You hate what you look like just as much as I hate what I look like. Maybe even more."

I couldn't deny it. I hadn't taken my shirt off in public since fifth grade, and even then it was because I'd stepped in an ant bed.

"That's different," I said. "That's—"

"No. It's *not* different. Maybe you're right, JT. Maybe you *are* fat. And I'm fat too. And we should just go off and live in a town for fat people where nobody can make us feel worse about ourselves than we already do."

I wanted to remind her that we *did* live in a town for fat people, by which I meant the state of Florida, but she had already stormed off to the car. I felt guilty that I'd allowed my lack of confidence in myself to make Heather question my confidence in her. Her logic made sense. If I was so down on my own body, how could I not be down on hers, which was at least twice my size?

"You ready?" Seth called from the gas pump with his bright smile and perfect gay guy body that could make any shirt look as good as it did on the mannequin in the store.

"Yeah. Coming," I said.

Neither Heather nor I said a word about any of this to him. It was our own little fat, self-loathing secret.

As we crossed into Virginia, it began to get dark. Having never left Florida before, I found it weird to see just how much the rest of the country looked like the rest of itself. When you're on an interstate, you're basically seeing the same empty fields and billboards for guns over and over and over. And off the interstate, it's the same chain stores and strip mall setup. America the beautiful.

Just as it became dark enough for Seth to turn on the

headlights, there was loud sort of boom, rip, then the sound of our screeching tires as Seth pounded the brakes.

"What the hell?" Seth shouted as he jumped out of the car. Heather and I watched as he said, "Oh crap. This is bad. This is really bad."

Seth was running his hands through his hair. Lit by the red of the car's flashers, he looked like a pop star in a music video. I got out to join him. One of our back tires was flat. In fact, it was worse than flat—it was a pile of rubber.

Seth, it seemed, had also deflated to a pile of rubber. "My dad's going to kill me. Literally. Will you speak at my funeral, JT? Heather? Will you sing?"

I bent down to assess the damage. It was bad.

"Do you have a spare?"

Seth shook his head. "No. I think that *was* the spare."

He kicked a rock, which skidded across the completely empty highway. It echoed into the darkness, creating a spooky sensation of just how far away from home we really were. We were on one of those old back highways because our GPS was taking us on a shortcut. A GPS can really solve all your problems— except, of course, for a flat tire.

"Should we call 911?" Heather asked as she got out of the car.

"What? No. That's not what people do about flat tires."

Heather shrugged. "We could get it towed into town and fixed in the morning, but that's going to cost a lot of money. How much money do we have left?"

Seth kicked one of the not-flat tires in frustration. It was rare for me to see Seth lose his cool.

"Not enough," he muttered. "Crap. This was a terrible idea, wasn't it?"

"What was?" I asked.

"This. Lying to our families and driving all the way to New York for . . ."

"For me?"

Seth stopped. He knew he'd said the wrong thing.

"No. That's not what I mean at all. I'm sorry. That came out wrong."

"No—you're right. We wouldn't be doing this if it wasn't for me needing a stupid scholarship."

Seth grabbed my hands. "But I want to help you do that. That's why I—"

I yanked away.

"Why? Why do you want to help with that, Seth? I mean, if everything is temporary, why do you care about helping me? Sooner or later, I'm just going to be some memory from high school—a chubby, not-so-bright, stuck-in-Florida memory, who can't ever, as you say, live in the moment, while you go off and experience some awesome, perfect life far away."

"Hey. Don't say that."

"You don't get it! You're perfect; you never have to worry about stuff that upsets you."

"STOP SAYING THAT. I am *not* perfect. That's *so* not fair! There is plenty that's upsetting me RIGHT THIS VERY MINUTE. And I never said we were temporary. I just said—"

"But you did! Last night you did."

"I just meant that we can't overthink things because it takes us out of the moment, JT. Jesus Christ, can't you ever just calm down for one second and not immediately overreact."

"What?!"

Heather stepped in between us. "JT, calm down. You *are* overreacting a bit. You're upset, just—"

"Oh! Me?! *I'm* overreacting, Heather? You're the one who had a complete meltdown at the gas station earlier because some creep we met at a diner called you fat!"

Heather's face fell, as if I'd just punched a kitten in front of her.

"Screw you," she said, quietly and painfully. "I told you that in private. I told you that because you're just as bad about hating yourself as I am and I knew you'd understand."

"Wait. What happened?" Seth asked.

Heather shook her head, turned her back to me, and spoke solely to him.

"That guy Mark told me that the reason he was into me was because he'd never been with a fat girl before. Only people who were 'normal.' I didn't want to make a big deal about it—the absolute last thing I want is to be the stereotypical fat girl who's freaking out about her weight to two gay guys on the side of a country road."

Seth turned to me. "JT, see? This is yet another reason you need to be kinder to yourself. How can your best friend trust your encouragement when you can't even it trust it yourself?"

"You know what? You were right. This *was* a terrible idea. Let's just throw in the towel right now, call your mommy and daddy, and tell them the whole story so they can fly us back to

Tampa and forget all about this stupid scholarship or my stupid future!"

A pair of headlights came shining from down the road. We stopped. This could be either help or an ax murderer, and I wasn't sure which we needed more. The car pulled up and the window rolled down. The two people inside didn't look like ax murderers . . . but it's hard to tell with ax murderers; they don't really have a traditional "vibe." This was an older couple, grandparental in their demeanor.

"You kids all right?" the man asked with a deep southern drawl.

"It's our tire." Seth pointed at the very flat problem.

"Yikes!" the man said, peering out the window for a look-see. "That thing's seen the last of the road, I'd say."

The woman leaned forward; she was very pretty. Her hair was red with streaks of white, and very big. There was something familiar about her.

"Y'all from around here?" she asked.

The three of us looked at one another, waiting for someone to answer. None of us wanted to admit to being miles and miles away from home to two strangers on an empty dark highway. However, none of us wanted to be stranded either. I spoke up.

"No. We're from Florida, we—"

"Florida?" The woman reacted as if I'd said *Budapest*. "Good lord, y'all *are* far away from home. What are you doing all the way up here in Virginia?"

"We're on our way to New York for a competition. It's for a scholarship. I'm—"

I stopped myself, realizing that it also might not be the best idea to admit to being on my way to a drag queen pageant in the middle of a dark road in Virginia.

The man's accent was so southern it was basically deep fried and covered in gravy. "Y'all got anybody around here you can call?"

I explained that we didn't, and before I could ask about a nearby motel, the woman was offering to let us come stay at their farm, as if she'd known us her entire life.

"It's just right down the road," she said. "It's a big house and we've got an apartment above the garage, so you won't even have to be around us old folk. Come, stay the night, and we'll figure out what to do with your tire in the morning. Y'all don't have any business sitting out here all by yourselves. And the only repair shop around here closes as soon as Foster passes out drunk, which is usually about three hours ago. I'd call him, but that would only wake him up, and you never want him working on your car when he's pissed—in both senses of the word. You're much better off with us."

I couldn't believe it. It's clichéd to say, but there really *are* some good people left in the world, and though I didn't even know these people's names, I somehow knew they were some of them.

"I'm Tina; this is Bud."

Tina smiled a big sweet smile at us. Again, something seemed familiar.

"I'm JT. This is Seth and Heather."

Seth and Heather both said hello, looking to me with slight concern. Were we actually going to get into the car with these strangers? Before my mind could answer, Bud was helping Seth put our suitcases into their car and Tina was asking if were hungry.

"Yes!" Heather responded, obviously quicker than she had meant to. Then, looking over at me, she attempted to stifle a guilty grin. "Shut up."

I was so happy to have her speaking to me that I did exactly what she said.

# chapter **eleven**

"SORRY 'BOUT THE MESS," TINA said, throwing her coat over the sofa as soon as we got into the house. The place was far from messy—cluttered, yes, but messy, no. It was one of the biggest houses I'd ever been in, and everywhere you looked your eye landed on something homey and interesting. Like a Cracker Barrel without the overt sense of bigotry.

"Bud. You go fix them something to eat. I've got that sweet potato casserole in the fridge. I'll show y'all to the garage apartment."

Tina led us into the massive backyard. A giant pool was covered in one of those green pool covers nobody ever uses in Florida. The apartment sat above a four-car garage, with stairs snaking around its side. The whole walk there, Tina's big red hair didn't move even once.

"It ain't much, but it's something," she said, flipping on the lights to reveal a place that was far from just something. The apartment was way bigger and way nicer than any apartment I'd ever been in. That's when I realized Tina was one of those people who always sets you up to be disappointed so that you'll always be pleasantly surprised. I appreciated that in a person.

"There's a room right there off the kitchen, and another one over yonder, and that sofa pulls out into a bed if you want it."

"This is so nice of you," I told her. "I don't know what to say—"

"Aw, don't give it another thought. We never use this place anyway. If it were up to Bud, it'd be his sanctuary to come watch football without my complaining about it. But I like having him for company. Y'all get comfortable. I'm going to make sure he hasn't set the house on fire trying to heat up that casserole."

Tina moved a mile a minute, so before we could even respond I could hear her high heels clapping their way down the stairs.

The tension from earlier returned the minute Tina left us alone. The way Tina had laid it out for us, it was clear she thought there weren't any couples here. And from the way Seth and I weren't speaking, maybe there weren't.

Right now, Seth was wandering over to peek into the other rooms. "This place is really, really nice," he reported without acknowledging the awkwardness between us.

Heather sat down on the sofa and immediately focused all her energy on her phone.

We all knew the silence was there. We were trying to pretend like we didn't, and we were very bad pretenders.

"So do we all hate one another?" I said, breaking the ice. Then I quickly added, "I don't hate either of you."

"Me either," Seth chimed in.

"I guess it would be a waste to be mad at one another in a place like this, huh?" Heather said, looking up from her phone.

"I know this is stressful—traveling always is—but can we all try and be a little nicer to one another?" Seth asked, timidly.

"No promises, bitch," Heather deadpanned.

All three of us laughed. It was the first time we'd genuinely laughed all day, and a wave of relief washed over me. They were my two favorite people on earth. Fighting with them hurt way more than whatever the issue was that we were fighting about to begin with. Sometimes the people you love the most are the most difficult for you to be around, because they see right through your crap and don't mind telling you. The truth was that I had overreacted on the road, and they were well aware that I tended to overreact quite a bit, but I didn't feel like getting into all that again. At least not in such a nice place.

"I mean, you guys . . . look at this!" I circled the room, checking out all the fancy furniture, artwork, and electronics. "Is this another bathroom?" I opened a closet and immediately began choking on something made out of bright blue feathers.

Seth rushed over. "Are you okay?"

I pulled my head out of the closet, three or four blue feathers falling out of my mouth.

"What the hell is in there?" Seth asked, watching the feathers fall onto the floor.

"I don't know . . . but it's none of our business. I shouldn't have been looking anyway. It's—"

Before I could finish my sentence, Seth had yanked open the

closet doors, revealing a roomful of costumes. And not just any costumes—incredibly old, colorful, shiny costumes.

"Holy Mary, Mother of God!" Seth cried out. "We're the Gayders of the Lost Ark."

Heather barreled in just in time to see the bedazzled green pantsuit Seth was holding up to himself, his eyes the size of saucers.

"Guys," she said, "we shouldn't be going through their stuff—" But as soon as she saw what was inside, her warning fell flatter than our tire. "Are those costumes or just really old clothes?!" Heather gasped, pushing past me and picking up a hot-pink sequined number.

"These aren't costumes. These are works of art."

It was a museum—but it was a private museum, and I still felt like we were trespassing. "You guys. Stop. We don't know these people. We can't go through their—"

Before I could finish my sentence, my eyes fell on a plastic box in the corner.

"Wigs," I said breathlessly. "Lots of wigs."

Seth opened the box, pulling out just about every hair color I'd ever seen. I felt like we'd discovered lace-front, real-human-hair gold. I tried to compose myself.

"Guys," I said. "Seriously. She's coming back any minute with—"

Seth stood up, coming toward me with a long strawberry-blond wig that resembled my mom's hair from the back when she used to wash it.

"Are you two thinking what I'm thinking?"

His grin. Was so. Hard to. Resist. And so was the wig.

Still, I mustered my strength to say, "I'm thinking that we're invading someone's privacy. Put those fantastic, gorgeous, *perfect* wigs back."

I was really trying to be resilient. But Seth knew how to sabotage my resolve.

"JT," he said. "We have just stumbled upon the ultimate drag closet of all time."

Heather jerked her head around, the jet-black bob she was wearing bouncing along with her. "You mean Tina is a drag queen?!"

"What I mean is, this stuff is perfect for JT to wear in New York! These are Miss Drag Teen USA–winning clothes, not like the crappy, cheap clothes we brought."

Just then, I heard the clapping of Tina's heels coming back up the stairs. I panicked.

"Get that stuff back in the closet! GO!" I whispered as loudly as one can whisper without it not being whispering.

Seth and Heather furiously repacked the box . . . but it was too late. The door to the apartment was already opening and Tina was inside.

"Yoo-hoo! Anybody hungry—"

She stopped cold in the doorway, her eyes lowering to see the three of us attempting to shove all the costumes back into the closet. I braced myself for her reaction and made a mental note of how we'd gotten to the house, just in case she kicked us out without another word.

I was the first to jump to my feet, Heather and Seth following shortly thereafter.

I said, "We're all sorry!"

Tina's face was expressionless.

"We weren't snooping," Seth swore. "I mean, I guess we were, but when we saw one of those incredible pieces of fashion history sticking out of the closet—well, I personally couldn't have lived with myself if I hadn't looked at it!" Seth was revealing way more about himself than I wanted Tina and Bud to know.

"What kind of competition are y'all heading to New York for?" Tina's voice remained flat and quiet.

"Well, JT can't afford college and his parents are no help and I found this competition for—"

I stepped forward, stopping Seth before it was too late. "We can just go if you're upset. We never meant to—"

"Upset? Lord." Tina chuckled to herself. "I must seem pretty damn uptight!"

We all awkwardly chuckled along with her, the way people do in action movies when the bad guy makes a lame joke and laughs at it while holding a weapon.

Tina sighed. "It's official. I'm too old to be famous anymore, I guess."

Heather, Seth, and I looked at one another, confused.

Tina waited a beat for recognition to come. When it didn't, she smiled and said, "My name is Tina Travis. I used to sing country music, a million and two years ago. Back when the dinosaurs were around and somebody who looks like me could get internationally famous."

*Tina Travis.* As I rolled the name around my brain, her face and hair began to look more and more familiar. Then it hit me. She had the same face and unmovable hair as a woman on one of my mom's old records.

"Now," Tina said. "Let me guess. One of you must be a drag queen." She crossed her arms and smirked at us, striking the exact pose on the old record I'd just remembered. "Nobody alive today but a drag queen would see any of that junk as fashion history. That's why it's stuck up here and not at the Opry. Did you find the wigs?" Tina brushed past us, opening the closet and dragging out the box of wigs behind her. "Back when I used to tour, I'd mix things up every few songs. Nowadays I just stick with this one."

She scratched her head, shifting the immovable hair like a hat.

"So . . . which one of you wants to try one on?"

She held up a blond curly wig that reminded me of Taylor Swift after a long night. Without missing a beat, all three of us shot our hands in the air. Tina threw her head back and laughed. Her hair again didn't move. Not even once.

We dug through the wig box for over an hour, all four of us forgetting the sweet potato casserole and our problems entirely. Tina exuded the kind of charm you only saw from famous people. Or rather, the kind of charm I imagined you only saw from famous people. She made each of us feel like we were the most interesting person in the room, even though the whole time she was *way* more interesting than any of us.

"And what do you have to do to win this thing?" she asked me now, styling the long strawberry-blond wig on top of my head.

"It's a few outfits, an interview, and a speech about why drag matters to you."

"No talent?!" Tina gasped, spilling a bunch of bobby pins onto the floor. Seth intervened, looking adorable in a wig three times as big as his head. (In the wig's defense, Seth has a very small head.)

"He has to do a talent, he's just in denial about it. We're going to figure out something."

"Well, damn. You better get to figuring."

I could feel my face blushing. I had no talent—that was the problem with figuring out my talent.

"He's going to sing," Heather said with a smile.

"I am NOT going to sing."

Tina grinned and looked down at me. "Why not?"

"Because I don't sing. I can't."

"Sure you can. Everyone can sing."

"I really can't—"

"He sang a song from *The Little Mermaid* in front of our whole school," Heather tattled. "It was amazing until the power failed and he got booed off the stage."

" 'Part of Your World'?" Tina asked me.

I nodded.

She seemed satisfied by this answer. "Now you stop and come with me to my music room. All of you, bring a wig!"

Seth and Heather stood up to follow her.

But I stayed down. "No. Really. I can't. I don't want to humiliate myself in front of you. Let's just—"

Before I could finish, Tina was pulling me up from the floor, revealing an impressive amount of strength for such a petite old woman.

I had no choice but to follow her.

Tina's fame and success were fully revealed in her music room. Her piano was covered in Grammys and other shiny gold statuettes that reflected gold speckles of light on her face while she sat at the piano.

"I've got the perfect song for something like this," she told me. "And I wrote it, so you better like it or you're all out on the streets." She paused while I laughed nervously. "It's a joke. Lord! You better find some humor before you get to New York is all I have to say. Sugar, hand me that yellow book right there."

Heather handed her a yellow book filled with sheet music. Tina flipped her way through it, doing that thing where she licked her finger in order to turn the pages faster. I'd never seen anyone actually do that in real life before. We all stood around her piano, wearing our favorite wigs.

"Here it is! Now. Listen."

I looked over at Seth and we locked eyes. He mouthed, "You can do this."

*Easy for you to say, bitch.*

Tina began to play, the song beautiful and beautifully familiar.

As she began to sing, the gorgeous sound of her voice made so many memories come rushing back. Of course I knew her music. Everyone did. Tina Travis wasn't just *some* country singer. At one point she had been *the* country singer.

She continued to play and sing the song, a ballad called "People Care." She purred the lyrics and looked up at me with a twinkle in her big green eyes.

> *Tried before and I failed.*
> *Thought I knew, but that boat sailed.*
> *Tried to find the real me*
> *and I just couldn't see.*
> *Now every day is a blessing,*
> *every day a new try,*
> *a chance to find yourself,*
> *find the reason why.*
> *People care about me,*
> *which I sometimes forget.*
> *People care about me,*
> *and that's as lucky as you get.*

The melody was catchy, soft, sweet, and a little corny—the kind of music that gets not just into your head but in your veins and blood. As I looked around the room at Seth and Heather, listening so intently, I realized that the song was right. People *did* care about me. Even after I'd argued with both of them hours earlier, they still cared.

*People care about me,*
*which I sometimes forget.*
*People care about me,*
*which is as lucky as you get.*

We all sang along, and just as we reached the final chorus, I was so lost in the song, singing full out, that I didn't notice everyone else had stopped singing until it was over. Tina turned around on the piano bench and looked at me with a big smile.

"Can't sing, my ass," she said, handing me the sheet music.

I hadn't found my talent. It had been given to me, by people who cared.

# chapter **TWELVE**

"WITH A VOICE LIKE YOURS, I'll kill you if I ever catch you smoking a cigarette. You hear me, boy?" Tina commanded as she rocked in a rocking chair on her front porch, smoking her third consecutive cigarette. Heather had gone to bed and Seth had insisted on cleaning up the dishes from dinner, which Tina hadn't put up much of a fight about. "You worry a lot, don't you?"

"Huh? How can you tell?" I laughed; she'd thrown me off guard.

"I can see it in your eyes: worry worry worry. I ain't wrong, am I?"

I shrugged. She wasn't.

"I knew how to sing from the time I could talk. As a point of fact, my mama said I could sing *before* I could talk. She said I'd sit up in my crib all night long just singing up a storm, and they felt bad making me stop because I sounded so good." She took a long swig from a bottle of beer. "But you want to know what? It wasn't until I was twenty-nine years old that I sang in public."

"Come on! That can't be true."

As she shook her head, the porch light created little beams in the cigarette smoke circling her head, like heavenly rays.

"Sure was. I'd sing in a studio at the piano, back when I was just writing songs. I'd play a song for Loretta or Tammy or, worse yet, Dolly damn Parton."

"What's the problem with Dolly Parton?"

Tina rolled her overly made-up eyes. "She stole my act."

"Huh?"

"I was white trash with big boobs and bad wigs long before Dolly was—she just perfected it." She pointed her long finger in my face. "Look it up."

"Is that why it took you so long to sing?"

She threw her hands in the air. "Lord, no! Dolly was the last thing that kept me from performing. I was absolutely dying to show *her* who was boss!" She paused, waiting for me to reply. "*Me*, by the way."

I nodded.

"I was terrified of singing. Everybody'd say, Tina, you ought to be the gal singing this one, and I'd get all flustered and change the subject. 'Cuz the truth was I wanted to, but I was scared."

"But you knew you could sing."

"Sure, I *knew* I could, but that didn't mean I wasn't afraid of doing it. There's a big difference between being able to do something and actually doing something." She finished her beer in another long swig, put it down, and grabbed my hand. "You've got something, JT. I saw it by that piano tonight. I watched you find it; now all you have to do is not forget it's in you."

She patted my knee and we sat there in silence for a while, just the sound of crickets chirping across the big field in front of us.

"Can I tell you something?" I said, breaking the silence.

"Go right ahead."

"Earlier, when I was singing at the piano, when I didn't realize I was singing all by myself? It was the most 'in the moment' I've ever felt."

She smiled a big Cheshire cat sort of grin. "That's called passion, sugar. And it feels good, huh?"

"You know how people talk about being in the moment? Well, I thought that maybe I was the exception. That nothing could put me in the moment, but tonight I felt it. I felt like I was really, truly there. Does that sound silly?"

"I think it's the least silly thing you've said all night."

In a lot of ways, Tina reminded me of my nana. They didn't look anything alike and their lives couldn't have been more different, but they'd grown up in similar eras and conditions, and somehow became the best versions of themselves they could be. Like Nana, Tina didn't grow up with much, but unlike Nana, she ended up with a lot. At the end of the day, however, they both valued loving themselves and those around them above anything else. And when Tina squeezed my hand, her hand was soft and wrinkled, old, like Nana's.

I pulled the page out of my pocket and glanced down at the word *talent*.

"What's that you got there?"

"It's the list, for the pageant. Glamour, talent, heart, and soul."

She took the napkin and examined it, squinting her old eyes to make out Seth's handwriting.

"Seems you've already got one crossed out. Glamour, huh? How'd you find that? Seeing me?" She chuckled a deep laugh that turned into a cough.

"This drag queen in South Carolina," I explained. "She gave me a makeup lesson and made me look amazing. Like, I genuinely felt beautiful. Look."

I pulled out my phone and opened up the photo I'd taken with Bambi. I handed it over to Tina. She smiled at it.

"How about that."

"I know. I don't even look like myself."

She shook her head. "Naw. I think you're showing yourself completely. See that smile, JT? That's what's inside of you, and it's just waiting for you to reach in there and touch it. Well, symbolically, that is."

I looked back at the photo. She was right—my smile was different. It was the happiest I'd ever seen myself in a photo. There was no fear, no tension, no nerves. Just joy.

"Your parents cool?" she asked, after a moment.

"What do you mean?"

"They cool? Like with the gay stuff, the drag stuff, all of that stuff people get bent out of shape about for no reason."

The word *cool* sounded so silly coming out of her mouth.

"Yeah, they're fine with it," I told her. Then, because that didn't feel like the most honest picture, I added, "They don't really think about me much. When I told them I was gay, they reacted the same as when I've ever told them anything."

"Which is?"

"A non-reaction, basically. They have their lives, their routines, their business, each other. They don't really need me. They never have."

Tina pushed her cigarette stump out into an old ashtray in the shape of Elvis sitting beside her, and immediately lit a new one.

"Everybody needs their kids, JT."

I shrugged. I didn't have a response to that because I wasn't sure if that was actually true.

"They do," Tina insisted. "Even your parents. They might not *get* you, but they need you. What do they do?"

"They run my grandpa's old gas station down in Clearwater. It's right outside Tampa. Barnett's Oil and General Store."

"I see. And what do they think about the pageant?"

I explained that they didn't know, and about how we hadn't told them about coming to New York and had actually lied about going to spring break in Daytona instead.

"They didn't want more details?"

"Nope."

Tina processed this for a moment.

"Well, I'll tell you this. My own mama *hated* the idea of me going into music. Said I'd end up homeless and that she wasn't going to put another roof over my head once I came crawling back. She never really got over that mentality either—she was always so dismissive of my success when it eventually came. She swore it was fleeting, and insisted I had better save up because the day it all went away was coming, and coming soon. She never even came to see me perform."

"No. Come on!"

She shook her head, sucking on her (as she described it) cancer stick.

"Nope. Never came to see me. She had so many chances, but she always had some excuse or another. Too far to travel, she had quilt guild that night, she was sick, afraid of flying. It was always something."

"Didn't that hurt your feelings?"

She let out a loud "Ha!" that echoed off the pine trees into the night air.

"Of course it did! It just about killed me! But when she died, do you want to know what I found? Not one but *seven* scrapbooks full of every magazine or newspaper clipping that had ever mentioned my name."

"How did that make you feel?"

She let out a sigh and rocked back and forth in her chair for a while. "Disappointed, for both of us. She was too scared to celebrate me, and I was too scared to ask her to. And in the end, we never got a chance to undo that for either of us." She took another drag from the cigarette. "Life, ya know?"

"Uh-huh."

She pointed her long finger at me. "Let them in, even if they don't seem to want in. Ask 'em. Trust me. Someday you'll be glad you did."

We stayed sitting on the porch for a while, looking out at the big open sky. I knew it was high time that I decided to be nicer to myself, to allow the people who loved me to celebrate me. Just then, a big owl landed on the branch of the enormous old oak tree in the yard. It sat there, hooting, just like the one used to do at Nana's house. The universe's message was quite simple: Follow Nana, and Tina, and Bambi's leads and maybe, just maybe, I'd find my otherwise.

Bud drove into town, got a replacement tire, and had it changed before any of us had gotten up. We tried to pay him back but he refused; Tina said he was probably just happy to have something to do.

After cooking us a *very* large breakfast, Tina sent us on our way, but not without insisting we take a bag of costumes and wigs for the competition. I put them into my suitcase with the wigs and clothes we'd already packed. Those other queens might be going to the pageant with years of experience, but I had something none of them would have: a wig that had belonged to Tina Travis. Plus a green paisley pantsuit that zipped up the back and hugged my hips so perfectly that you'd have thought I'd been to a gym before. And a trash bag full of more outfits.

Before we said our good-byes, Tina pulled me aside. She held my chin in both hands and scratched a patch of stubble I'd missed the last time I'd shaved.

"Hm. Better get somebody to teach you how to shave better before you get to New York, sugar." She lowered her voice, turning me away from the others. "I want you to have something."

"No," I protested, "I can't take anything else from you. You've already given me all those costumes and wigs."

Tina waved off my words. "Don't get excited, it's nothing as important as wigs or costumes. It's just this."

She slipped something into the palm of my hand—a wad of cash.

"Tina! That's a lot of money!"

She yanked me away from the group and whispered into my ear, "Shush! Bud thinks I'm some kind of mess when it comes to money. This will be our secret."

I looked through the wad of cash in my hand. At first glimpse, I counted four one-hundred-dollar bills and at least a dozen or so twenties.

"Yeah, but this is a way more than a lot, Tina."

She rolled her eyes. "Don't mess with me, JT. Put that in your pocket and get yourselves a nice hotel room when you get to New York. That place eats money for breakfast. Treat yourselves; feel glamorous. After all, that's the whole point of living, right?"

I hugged her, her big red wig scratching my cheek. She smelled just the right amount of superstar and old lady to warm my heart.

"And how can I find out if you win?"

"Are you on Facebook?"

She arched her eyebrows, giving me an expression that said *What do you think?*

"All right. Well, text me." I took her phone and programmed my number into it. "Thank you, Tina Travis. For everything."

She kissed me on the cheek. I could feel the outline of her lipstick creating a track mark where her lips had been.

"Go win the damn thing," she said with the same big grin I'd seen on that old record of my mom's.

We returned to the group and said our good-byes. Then Seth, Heather, and I hit the road. We were back on the same highway where the whole tire debacle had begun the night before. Before we got back onto the interstate, I pulled the car over and cut off the engine.

"Don't tell me you have to pee already?" Heather asked.

"No. I just wanted to say I'm sorry." I looked at both of them. "I know I've been a bit of a handful these past few days."

"A bit?" Heather arched an eyebrow.

"Hey now, don't push me."

She laughed.

"But really, I'm sorry. I think I've been letting my nerves about this pageant bring out my every little dormant and not-so-dormant insecurity, and instead of trying to overcome them, I've just been feeding them with the self-hatred they need to keep controlling me."

"Wow. Okay, Oprah." Heather was taken aback. She added, "And that wasn't me calling you fat. Just ridiculously Zen and well spoken."

We all laughed and I cranked the car back up.

"Hey." Seth pinched my leg. "Thanks for saying that. I'm sorry too."

I smiled as I pulled the car back onto the interstate, and with my new wigs and costumes in the trunk and my two best friends at my side, we were off.

Seth was singing along to the radio as we passed a sign welcoming us into the state of Maryland. Suddenly he stopped singing and became quiet for a while.

"Has anyone called home since we left?" he asked, seemingly lost in some other thought.

None of us had. Heather had texted her mom sometime the day before, but otherwise we were completely cut off from the lives we knew. It was a neat feeling, with no one but the three of us knowing where we were. Arguably dangerous, but still a neat feeling. However, we decided we probably ought to call and at least pretend to update them.

The three of us paced back and forth around the car, each fabricating our own story about how spring break was going. Seth's dad was asking all sorts of details, telling him to have a blast. The good thing about having parents like mine is that you can lie to them at any time and they won't question you for a second, not because they think you're trustworthy but because they just don't care.

"Hello?!" My mom answered the phone in her usual sound of panic. For as long as I could remember, my mom had always answered the phone as if the house had just caught on fire.

"Hi. It's JT."

Li'l Biscuit yapped loudly over the sound of QVC in the background.

"Oh, hey. You still in Daytona? Don't tell me you got arrested or something!"

This was my mom's way of saying "How are you?"

"Nope. Not arrested. Daytona's fun. Just great. Really cool," I lied.

"Okay, so do you want something? Suzanne Somers is selling her three-way poncho right now and she's about to tell us the third thing it can do."

It was no surprise to hear my mom's lack of interest, but it was still a disappointment. Seth's and Heather's families had both gone on and on about how much they missed them, and the most my mom could say was that she needed to get back to some old TV actress selling a poncho that could be worn three different ways. (That said, I wanted to know more about this poncho myself.) I told Mom good-bye, she hung up without saying "I love you," and I rejoined the others by the snack machine.

"How'd it go?" Seth asked, pulling a bag of Lay's out of the machine.

"Fine."

"Did they quiz you like mine did?"

I gave Seth my *what the hell do you think?* look and he smiled.

"Well, consider yourself lucky that you didn't have to come up with a fake story about going to an all-you-can-eat fried shrimp buffet!" Heather shouted from the picnic table she was sitting on.

"Why would you make that up?" I asked.

"I don't know." She shrugged. "It was the first thing that popped in my head when they asked what I'd been up to. Speaking of which, is anyone else craving shrimp?"

Seth looked up from his phone. "Actually, since we're making pretty decent time, how would you guys feel about a detour?"

"To where?"

Seth was already mapping out directions. He seemed more tense than usual.

"It's a ways out of the way, but Ocean City, Maryland. Where we used to live before my dad moved us to Florida. I haven't been back in, what? I guess four years or something. Wow." Seth stopped and took in the passage of time. I could see how much he really wanted to go; it was sweet to see him trying not to sound too eager in case Heather and I protested.

"Why not?" I elbowed Seth in the hip. "It's important to live in the moment, you know?"

"Yeah," he said. "But I should warn you—the moment we're about to live in definitely belongs to the past."

And away we went.

# chapter THIRTEEN

IT WAS CLOUDY BY THE time we got to Ocean City. The town was located on the water but was nothing like a Florida town. It was a cold, quiet little place with small houses built around a large boardwalk that followed along the water's edge. We parked on the street and made our way over to the water and wandered down past the kind of places with T-shirts that read I'M WITH STUPID and an arrow pointing directly up. The whole place smelled more like a giant funnel cake than an ocean.

I knew this was where Seth had grown up—but I didn't know much more than that. The past was something he didn't talk about much—sometimes when there was a story from when he was a kid, but very little from his recent history. I didn't think about it much—my own sixth-, seventh-, and eighth-grade years weren't particularly compelling material either. I just assumed that Golden Boy Seth had been golden somewhere else, and then had left this place to come into my life.

"My dad and I used to come down here on Saturdays after Little League ball games and get either ice cream or pizza, or ice cream *and* pizza if my team had won," he said to me now. "Those were the best days."

A seagull flew overhead, pooping on the boardwalk, so close that the disgusting blob almost landed in my hair. I jumped, and both Heather and Seth burst into laughter.

"Shut up or I'm throwing one of you over the edge," I warned them.

A strong breeze blowing off the water had left the whole boardwalk uncrowded. Heather spotted a booth selling purses made out of recycled license plates—the kind that no one has carried since 2001—and she reacted like someone currently living in 2001. She walked over to check them out while Seth and I wandered toward the railing overlooking the water.

"Is it like you remember?" I asked.

"Sure. Sorta. There used to be more arcades and stuff, I think, but maybe it just seemed like there were a bunch because I was little."

"It's a pretty town."

Seth nodded, distracted by something.

"Everything okay?"

"Uh-huh." He paused with a slight frown. "Well, actually . . . you sorta hurt my feelings the other day."

"What? Really? I apologized for freaking out about that guy. I really believe that you weren't flirting with him and have fully let it go."

"No, not that. It was when you said everything was perfect for me. That I've never had anything to worry about or whatever." He was avoiding eye contact, focusing on a boat or barge way out in the foggy distance.

"Seth, you know I didn't mean that to upset you. I just meant you have your stuff together. You're not a constant ball of nerves like me. People like you fit in. Everybody likes you."

He snapped his focus toward me. "Just because I fit in doesn't mean I have my stuff together, JT. I know you think you know me, but you only know the part of me I show, okay?"

His eyes were weighted with hurt. They didn't twinkle the way they usually did—they were muted, gray, like mine. This was not the Seth I knew.

"I'm sorry," I said. "I shouldn't have said that. Forgive me?"

"Everyone has stuff they can't seem to shake no matter how hard they try. Everybody has stuff they're afraid of. Everybody has stuff that breaks their hearts."

His voice was so thin and strained. And I couldn't tell: Did he want me to ask what he meant . . . or was he saying that there was a private part of him that I didn't have access to yet, and that I'd just have to take his word for the pain that was kept inside? Also, I was wrestling with the knee-jerk reaction to be pissed off at him that he had the audacity to withhold anything he was afraid of.

"I really didn't mean to upset you like this," I told him. Then, delicately, I asked, "Do you want to talk about it?" This was the door I was opening for him. But hopefully my tone told him I wouldn't be hurt if he decided he didn't want to walk through it right now.

In response, he took my hand and pulled me behind him down the boardwalk.

"Follow me," he said.

The school Seth had grown up going to was situated across the street from the pier, which felt like really strange planning on the school's part. Looking up at Seth's old school's windows overlooking the ocean, I couldn't help but imagine the countless hours its students must have spent not listening to a thing their teachers said.

It was late afternoon during spring break, so the school was mostly empty and strangely still, spooky in the way schools can be when they aren't full of kids attempting to learn and blend in. Seth let us into the school's main hallway through the front door. A long glass case lined the entire expanse of the walls, filled with trophies, heavily posed group photos, and the kind of pointless high school knickknacks people hold on to under the notion that they'll matter to them after they're adults. I mean, really, who has ever said, "Wow. Thank God I held on to this plastic button that says Homecoming Planning Committee 2003!"

"So you went here for elementary school?" I asked, faking interest, the way one has to when being shown photos of something that seem to matter to the person who's showing the photos.

"And middle school. It's the only school I went to until we moved." Seth's attention was fixed on a photo of three nerdy-looking kids crowded around a chessboard; they looked thirteen or so, all three in the most awkward and most sudden of pubescent growth spurts. I leaned down to get a closer look, and saw the caption: CHESS CLUB. The photo might as well have been a photo ad for an organization called Dorks United. The three kids' names were printed under the caption: Carolyn Hedden, Ed Robson, and Steve Coulson.

Coulson. Like Seth Coulson. As I started at the photo longer, the pimply kid in the middle of the photo looked like he could be related to Seth somehow. That's when Seth spoke up.

"Recognize me?" He arched his eyebrows, nervously.

"What do you mean? That's not you. It says Steve Coulson. Wait . . . you have a brother?"

Seth shook his head and sighed.

"My name is Steve, not Seth. Or . . . it was a long time ago. And by a long time ago, I mean middle school."

It was my turn to arch my own eyebrows—not nervously, but in confusion. Seth went on.

"JT, I've never told anyone this before in my life . . . but when I was growing up here, I was like the biggest loser in school. My idea of a good time was playing chess and second-guessing every single aspect of my personality until I'd get a headache and go back to playing chess to distract myself."

"Wait," I interrupted. "Are you saying you changed your name because you were ashamed of playing chess? I mean, yeah, as far as board games go, it's boring as shit, but I don't think that warrants a name change."

Seth stared down at the peeling linoleum of the hallway. "Once my dad got his job in Florida and I was sure we were moving, I made the decision to start over. All my life I'd been the loser kid who didn't fit in. I didn't know how to dress, how to talk to people without sounding like a borderline psychopath. I just didn't know how to blend into the groove of things." He shrugged. "Then we had to move during my eighth-grade year and most people probably would've been so upset, but I was so excited. I knew it was my chance to start over. To hit refresh like I used to do on the computer games I'd spend my nights playing as a way to distract myself from having zero friends. Wow, did that sound as depressing as I think it did?"

This whole "coming out" monologue was coming out of left field in every possible way. So much so that I thought he was pulling my leg.

However, from the anxious look on Seth's face, I could tell this was no joke.

"I'm confused. You changed your name?"

"Do I seem like a Steven to you? With a V, no less."

I couldn't imagine Seth named anything but Seth. Especially not *Steven*.

"My parents were a little weird about it at first, Steven being a family name, but they knew how hard a time I'd had over the years and they finally gave in. I legally changed it and everything. It was really freeing. Plus, I didn't want the people who'd spent all of middle and elementary school making fun of me to be able to find me on Facebook. I basically counter-catfished myself."

This was a lot of information to take in. Seth was Seth, not Steven into Seth. My immediate reaction was to be angry with him for never telling me until this moment. However, there was something in Seth's eyes that I couldn't help but understand. Something that could sometimes feel like it only lived in me.

He went on. "I've never told anyone. Ever. Because I vowed that I'd leave Steven in my past and that Seth would always fit in and be liked. And you know what? He has." He spoke these words so honestly that one could ignore what might have normally seemed incredibly egocentric. "You find the person inside of you that makes you feel like yourself, or makes you feel whole, and that's who you have to take into the world."

I glanced back at the photo of Steven Coulson. Within his shy, sad eyes I saw the beginnings of Seth. The beginnings of the most special boy I'd ever met. And I wanted to ask a million questions, but all I could do was grab him, hold him as tight as possible, push my lips against his nervously sweaty forehead, and whisper:

"I love you, Seth or Steven or whoever the hell you want to be next. You're you, you've always been you, and I'm so lucky to love you."

He kissed me back.

"This is so weird. You. Here," he said. "Do you mind if I look around a little?"

"Not at all." I sensed this was something he had to do alone. "I'll go find Heather."

Perhaps he was hoping to heal whatever wounds were left behind by Steven, by experiencing the place as Seth this time around, or maybe he just wanted to binge out on his old chess set. I left him to do his thing and went back out to the pier. I found Heather attempting to avoid a conversation with a crazy man who had an actual cat on his head and was begging people to pay him for a photo. Heather was carrying a large shopping bag full of recent purchases: the license plate purse, a T-shirt, a stupid-looking hat, and a bunch of other crap she didn't need.

"Hey! Where's Seth?"

"In there." I pointed toward the school.

"He's inside a school on his spring break? What's he trying to prove?"

I explained the whole story to Heather as she stood there captivated. I couldn't believe it myself, even upon hearing it all a second time from my own mouth. I also couldn't shake the increasingly selfish feeling of being hurt because Seth had kept me out of his full life and truth. I wondered how different things would have been if I'd known Seth had been just as much of an outsider as me, once upon a time.

"So, literally nobody is perfect, huh?" Heather asked, with an air of surprise and slight trace of disappointment. "Y'know, it actually makes me feel a little bit better knowing that even Seth—gorgeous, smart, beloved Seth—has had something to cry about. Is that horrible?"

"Naw," I said. "At the end of the day, we're all just a bunch of freaks trying to pass for normal. And I reckon, it turns out, there is no such thing."

"I can't believe he's never told you. I mean, after all this time together," she said, slightly throwing the statement away, as if she hadn't wanted to point out the place where she knew my mind had already set up camp and was roasting marshmallows.

Seth walked out, his head held high, and joined us. We walked away from the school, all three of us holding hands and silent for a while.

"Are you okay?" I said. His hand was a trace sweatier than usual.

"Yeah. I am. I walked around, and just sorta pretended the last few years had never happened. I imagined that I'd never moved away or changed my name or whatever. I just came to terms with the fact that you can run, you can reinvent yourself, but you'll always be you. You know? And while that's a little scary, I guess it's also a little comforting too."

We embraced before walking for a ways, back toward the car, but before we left the boardwalk, I stopped.

"How would you feel about going to get pizza *and* ice cream?" I asked.

Heather and Seth ran along ahead, toward the pizza place with a crooked neon sign that appeared to have been broken since long before I was born. I watched them for a moment. Seth had flipped like a switch, immediately his confident and upbeat self again, filling Heather in on what had just happened. Heather did a good job of pretending to hear this story for the first time. I wanted to feel happy for him, for his facing his issue head-on, and allowing himself to come up for air immediately after. However, I couldn't help but wonder why he'd kept it all to himself while I poured out every insecurity and issue I'd ever felt in the past four years, why he was able to (in the words of Taylor Swift) "shake it off" so easily and why I'd never been able to shake anything off in my entire life. Perhaps I should take this as a lesson for my own self, to allow myself to be okay with my mistakes and the voices in my head who had nothing but cruel things to say about me. I'd always thought of Seth as strong, but to find the ability to shut up those voices? Well, that deserved some kind of medal. Or at least a giant hug, which for now would have to do.

# chapter FOURTEEN

SEEING THE SIGN THAT READ NEW YORK CITY—50 MILES gave me legitimate goose bumps. We'd been driving all day and into the night, and here we were. New York City was the most special place on earth and I didn't mind saying that, even as someone who had, up until that moment, never been there. It was where, if you had even the tiniest inkling to visit, you'd never be whole until you did. I didn't think New York City created interesting people—but I believed it told them it was okay to be interesting. Then, inevitably, paid them for it.

"Fifty miles," I said out loud, without realizing it. "Wow."

"I cannot believe this is really happening!" Heather screamed from the backseat. Seth was beaming; he'd been the image of contentment ever since we left Ocean City. As we approached, we put on the New York playlist Heather had created for this special occasion, containing every song about New York you could think of: that Alicia Keys song, the Liza one, the Sinatra one, even the Taylor Swift one.

None of us had been to New York before except for Seth, and even then he'd been two and didn't remember it. It felt like every story I'd ever heard of people entering New York City for the first time compared it to *The Wizard of Oz*—and at first I was like, *Okay, we get it, you're gay, have you seen any other movie?* But when I actually got there, I thought, *Gee, someone walking into the Emerald City* is *the closest thing to the magic of arriving in New York City as you'll ever find, so the comparison is necessary.* If I was frustrated at Seth for slipping back into his New Shiny Self, not talking about what had happened in Maryland, it subsided as the immaculate towering skyline got closer and closer.

Before I knew it, we were in the Holland Tunnel, underwater, on our way into the city itself. To enter New York City, you literally have to go above or under water, leaving the rest of the country as you know it, to enter that special kingdom. At that point all I wanted was to be there, to be out of the car and in the streets like a real New Yorker. As we exited the tunnel, I rolled down my window. I wanted to smell the New York air.

"Ahhhh! We're here!" I cried out. "We're here! Let's take in the beauty of it all!"

Heather winced. "It smells like dog pee."

She was right. In unison, we all rolled our windows back up.

We were greeted with insane traffic, bumper to bumper, honking, people screaming in languages I'd never even heard before. Everyone seemed so pissed off—it was everything I'd ever dreamed of. Glowing billboards for Broadway shows and fancy clothing stores shone high above our car as we inched our way into this tiny island I'd always dreamed of stepping foot on.

I had made it. I had actually made it.

It wasn't until we were on our way down Eighth Avenue, past taxis and hordes of people coming out of Broadway shows, that Seth asked where we were headed.

"I mean, I know there are lots of hotels . . . but do we have one? I didn't think about that. I just sorta assumed we'd show up and stay somewhere."

I shushed him, turning down Judy Garland as she sang "*I like New York in June, how about you?*"

"You name it, we can stay there!" I announced with immense excitement.

"Huh?" Heather asked.

"Tina gave me some money—*a lot* of money—and she told me to put us up somewhere really nice." I pulled out the wad of cash from Tina and showed it to them. Both Heather's and Seth's eyes widened so much they looked like they might fall out.

"Holy crap," Heather whispered, almost religiously. "We're *totally* ordering room service."

Heather and Seth did a quick search, Googling *fancy New York hotels*. There were plenty of them, but none of the fanciest ones had available rooms for the night.

"Look up where Jennifer Aniston stays," I said.

"Why?" Heather asked, looking up at me in a beam of blue light from her phone.

"I don't know. I just think she has nice taste."

Heather couldn't argue—you could accuse Jennifer Aniston of a lot of things, but bad taste wasn't one of them.

Seth was already on it. "Apparently, somewhere called the Gramercy Hotel? Jesus! These rooms are six hundred bucks a night! How much money does Jennifer Aniston *have*?!"

"A lot!" I turned onto Thirty-Fourth Street just because I'd heard of it. "Fine, try someone a little *less* classy."

"Jessica Simpson?" Heather offered from the backseat.

"Perfect!"

Jessica Simpson's go-to hotel was booked, and by the time half an hour had passed, we'd checked the favorite New York hotels of Jennifer Hudson, Emma Stone, Kerry Washington, and, in one moment of desperation, Ariana Grande. Finally, we settled on a place where Seth's web results insisted Justin Bieber had gotten into a fight with Orlando Bloom. We figured that was fancy enough for us.

The farther downtown we got, the more confusing New York became. The streets, once simply named Thirty-First, Thirty-Second, Thirty-Third, etc., suddenly turned into names like Crosby, Houston, Mulberry. We finally found the hotel, and as we pulled up to the front, a fancy-looking man in a uniform came out, asking us if we were guests of the hotel and offering to park our car. I'd never seen anything like this in my life, just driving up to a door and handing your keys over to someone in a vest that's supposed to indicate they work there. Heather, trying really hard to seem unfazed by the whole situation, claimed the man was called a *valet*—which we later learned you don't pronounce the *t* in.

This was a whole new world.

Inside the hotel, it was dark and moody—a little too dark, to be honest. I didn't know how more people weren't bumping into things. I wondered what the whole point of making a room look nice was, if you were going to make it so dark you could barely see it. Everyone in the lobby, whether at the front desk or at the bar to the side, looked like an extra from a present-day version of *Sex and the City*. With its subtle hints of burning woods and the fancy soap I was inevitably going to steal from the hotel room, the place even *smelled* cool. There was a DJ elaborately set up in the corner who didn't even appear to be DJ-ing. Next to him was a really stunning supermodel reading a book inside a glass tank as if she were a really pretty fish.

Heather claimed she needed to pee, but I knew she probably just wanted to see how fancy the bathrooms were. Seth and I went to the desk to check in.

"Good evening. Name on the reservation?" the lady at the desk asked, peering over some skinny black glasses. She didn't smile—in fact, she seemed to be putting great effort into her avoidance of doing so.

"Hi. We just called a few minutes ago. We're—"

"The ones with the *Florida* area code?" She said the word *Florida* the way one would refer to a drowned water moccasin that's gotten stuck in a pool skimmer. At that moment, I didn't blame her. That's what the state seemed like to me, from far away.

"That's right," I said. "We just need the one room, two double beds, please."

My politeness seemed to annoy her. "ID, please," she said curtly.

I handed over my ID. She leaned over her iPad typing, her long jet-black bangs covering her eyes as she did so.

"How will you be paying for this?"

"Cash."

She looked up, her bangs falling perfectly back into place.

"We'll need a card on file."

I looked at Seth. None of us had a credit card.

"Well." Seth cleared his throat, attempting to cover his panic. "Can we give you a cash deposit instead?"

"No," she replied with zero emotion whatsoever. We were quiet for a moment while we tried to come up with what to say next.

"Is there any other option besides a card that we—"

"No." She cut us off, this time with seemingly *even less* emotion, which I hadn't thought was possible. "No hotel in New York is going to check you in without a credit card on file, Mr. . . ." She looked down at my ID, frowned condescendingly, then handed it back to me. "You should know that all New York hotels require an adult signature for people under eighteen."

Heather skipped up to the desk, delighted. "The bathroom has free mouthwash! Smell my breath!"

She opened her mouth really wide against my face, appalling the front desk lady. I stepped away.

"We'll be right back. We just need to discuss a, uh, matter, briefly."

Heather and Seth followed me over to a table by the bar. We sat down.

"Sorry! Should I not have made you smell my breath?" Heather asked, guiltily looking back over at the front desk.

"No. I mean, yes, that was disgusting, but that's not the problem," I said, fiddling with the wad of cash in my hand. "They require a credit card on file to check in, and hotels won't check you in if you're under eighteen. Why didn't we think of this ahead of time?" I was spiraling, the way I tended to do, allowing one thing to bring down everything else around it, the fatal addition to the house of cards my emotions lived in.

"Calm down, JT. It's going to be okay." Seth rubbed the top of my hand. "We will figure this out. Let's be rational. What hotel will let three underage teenagers with a wad of cash stay without asking questions?"

"We could go get a fake ID, open up a credit card in its name, and come back?" Heather offered.

I shot her a level glance. "A. That's called fraud. And B. How is that going to help us tonight?"

"Okay, okay. Wait. I've got it." Seth was looking down at his phone. "We'll call the pageant organizers and ask for help. They'll have to understand, right?"

"Great idea, Seth! Who's listed as in charge?"

"Someone named . . . Lady Rooster."

Heather rolled her eyes. "She sounds responsible."

"There's a phone number too." Seth was already dialing. "It's ringing! You talk to her—you're the contestant."

He handed me the phone. It rang for a long time without

going to voice mail. Just as I was going to hang up, someone answered. All I could hear was really loud background noise, as if the person was inside some kind of mob.

"HELLO?" the voice shouted over the noise. "WHO IS THIS?"

I tried to talk loud enough for the person to hear me but not so loud that I caused a scene in the hotel.

"Is this Lady Rooster?" I asked.

"YEAH," she bellowed.

"Hi. I'm JT Barnett. I'm in the pageant, the John Denton Foundation one, and we just got to New York but we don't have anywhere to stay because—"

The background noise was only getting louder, but Lady Rooster had enough lung strength to interrupt me. "I'M WORK-ING AND IT JUST GOT BATSHIT BUSY. CAN YOU CALL ME BACK OR JUST COME DOWN HERE?"

"WHERE'S HERE?" I shouted. Some of the lobby patrons looked at me like I'd let loose an epic verbal fart.

"XXXL! WHERE THE HELL ELSE DO YOU THINK I'D BE?"

She hung up before I could ask anything else.

"Well?" Seth asked, hopeful.

"Sounds like we're going somewhere called XXXL."

Our adventure, it seemed, had gotten just that large.

# chapter FIFTEEN

WE WEREN'T CRAZY ABOUT DRIVING again in Manhattan, so we left the car where it was and took a mind-blowingly expensive cab over to the mysterious-sounding XXXL, which turned out to be a not-so-mysterious enormous gay club. And when I say enormous gay club, I mean *really* enormous, like the Epcot of gay bars. Even from outside I knew this was going to be a lot for me to handle; if the tiny dive in South Carolina had sent me into a dramatic tailspin of insecurity, I imagined this place would ignite a hurricane. A line was wrapped around the building, full of ridiculously attractive gay men.

"This line will take hours, you guys," Seth said, surveying just how far down the block the parade of gays went. "Let's try going to the front and asking for Lady Rooster."

"We can't break in line!" I panicked. "These people will kill us. Besides, that guy at the door is checking IDs. They're not going to let any of us in there."

"Call Lady Rooster back and tell her we're outside."

Heather was laughing. "Is anyone else aware of how ridiculous it is that we keep having to say the name Lady Rooster in a serious way?" She shook her head in awe. "Gay people are great."

I tried calling Lady Rooster again but didn't get an answer. I sent a text—*Hey. This is JT who called earlier. We're outside the club*—but she didn't reply. We waited for half an hour as the line got shorter and shorter. Most of the guys checked out Seth on their way in, and I tried not to notice, deciding I had enough to worry about for one night. Finally, a side door was kicked open with a sharp orange heel; then a ball of orange and red feathers poked out. After a second I realized there was a face in the middle of it. From the costume alone, there was no question that this was Lady Rooster.

"You!" She pointed at me. "You the one blowing up my phone?"

I sheepishly walked over to her.

"Yeah, I'm JT Barnett. I'm in the pageant and we just got to town and we don't have anywhere to stay and—"

"Ugh. I'm on in five minutes. Lady Rooster doesn't normally let girls back here, but just stand where nobody can see you," she spat, giving Heather a less than welcoming look. "Get your asses in here."

She darted back inside, moving slightly like an actual rooster. I wasn't sure whether it was intentional or the product of the enormous cocktail she clutched in her talonlike fingers. We followed her into a grungy hallway, the graffitied walls literally pulsating from the loud music in the club. At the end of the hall was a large room crammed full of decorations for every possible holiday, and a tower of beer kegs.

I heard an announcer revving up the crowd, introducing the host of the evening's party, the one and only Lady Rooster. The crowd was going wild.

"You three wait here—and if you steal anything, Lady Rooster will know it." She touched up her lipstick in a cracked mirror taped to the wall. "And STAY OFF MY STAGE!"

With something that sounded eerily like an authentic rooster call, she was out the door and onto the stage, the audience going even wilder.

All three of us looked at one another and mouthed, "WTF?"

From the crack in the door, we watched Lady Rooster greeting the audience.

"Hello, New York! Who's ready to play a little chicken?!" She spoke with one of those vaguely British accents that is sometimes there and sometimes not. "This one goes out to all of Lady Rooster's fans! Are there any Chickadees in the house?" From the response, one could tell there were. "All right, then. Let's do this."

An old but familiar disco song played and the crowd cheered as Lady Rooster did an amazing job lip-synching the whole thing. She danced all over the place, pulled hot guys out of the audience, downed people's drinks, and, in a grand finale, shot a cannon full of orange and red feathers all over the crowd. As the feathers rained down on the hundreds of screaming fans, she made a dramatic exit offstage, directly back toward us.

I was amazed. Not just by what she pulled off, or the confidence that powered her considerable strut. But the way she had the audience eating out of her hand, like they were indeed little chicks and she was a goddess—that, I knew, was what I wanted to do. Not her way, but my way . . . whatever that way might be.

"You see that?" She blotted the sweat from her forehead with a towel. "That one number just got Lady Rooster a thousand bucks and unlimited cocktails all night. Who are you three again?"

She plopped down into a recliner. I stepped forward, as if I were meeting a foreign dignitary.

"I'm in town for the pageant, and you were listed as the contact, and we don't have anywhere to stay because we're underage and don't have a credit card."

"Dammit. Why the hell is Daryl listing me as the contact on his dumb charity fund-raiser?" she mumbled to herself as she pulled off her shoes and rubbed her feet. "Lady Rooster is the HOST of the damn thing, not the CONTACT, and she's not even wild about that. It's the *one* charity gig she does all year, unlike the rest of the queens in this town. They'll throw on their wig and go out there for just about any cause you can think of. But me? Bitch, I'm a career girl and don't you forget it!"

"I'm sorry if we"—*do not say ruffled your feathers, do not say ruffled your feathers*—"have inconvenienced you," I said.

"Listen, JP."

"It's JT."

"Whatever. JT and super twink and whoever this sidekick chick is—Daryl is my boyfriend. Ugh, husband now, actually. The prick made me marry him last summer. I told him I needed time, but he thought fifteen years had been enough; oh well.

Lady Rooster got a trip to Belize out of it and some new Fiestaware. Anyway, the pageant is his thing. He runs that foundation, the John Denton thing. You should talk to him. Not me."

Lady Rooster agreed to call Daryl, and when she reached him, she explained, in her crass manner, what was going on. She asked him to come downstairs. Apparently they lived around the corner.

"Two of them are your type," she told him. "The other has boobs."

"Why is she being so mean to me?" Heather whispered to us.

"Rooster!" A tough-looking—but kinda hot in an older, scary way—bouncer popped in. "Go give them an encore."

Lady Rooster cocked her head to the side. "What the hell do you think I am? Some kind of show pony? You slip me three hundred bucks cash and I'll give 'em one more, but that's it. Lady Rooster's feet are *killing* her." She casually looked over at me. "I hosted a drag brunch this morning. Apparently that's a thing now."

The bouncer agreed and handed her some cash as his eyes fell on Heather. It was clear he liked what he saw—and it was also clear he was at least ten years older than any of us. It was even more clear that Heather liked what *she* saw and was ignoring the fact that he was ten years older than any of us. They smiled at each other.

"I'm Roger," he said, ignoring the rest of us.

"Heather."

There was a knock on the door to the alley.

"That's Daryl. Open it, super twink," Lady Rooster commanded Seth.

"I've never seen you here before, have I?" Roger inched his muscular body toward Heather. Heather blushed as she shook her head, which only seemed to turn Roger on even more. Seth opened the door to the alley and a man I assumed was Daryl walked in. Immediately Roger stiffened away from Heather.

Daryl was a friendly teddy bear of a guy in his forties. He had a sweet smile, gray beard, and soft eyes—the complete opposite of his betrothed.

"I hear we got some homeless drag teens in here?" he said.

The announcer in the club was introducing Lady Rooster and her encore. "DAMMIT!" she screamed. "SOMEBODY could have given me a warning!" She shoved her heels back on and stomped back onto the stage. I thought she'd be huffing and puffing at the audience, but the moment before she hit the stage, all the rocky parts turned into diamonds. *There's something to be learned here*, I thought as I watched her start her number, flawless. She left all the crap going on in her life off the stage where it belonged. All that mattered up there was owning the room, and she certainly did that. I would have followed her from start to finish, but I sensed Daryl next to me, waiting to introduce himself. When I turned to him, I saw he'd noticed me noticing Lady Rooster in awe . . . and this got a smile from him, one that could only come from somebody who'd been with Lady Rooster through thick and thin.

"I'm Daryl Hart," he said.

"Hi, I'm JT. We just drove up from Florida—"

"JT Barnett?"

I was a little taken aback that he, or anyone in New York City for that matter, would know my last name.

"Um. Yes?"

He gave me a big bear hug. "Welcome to New York! And who are your friends?"

I introduced Seth, and he greeted him with a hug just as friendly and warm as the one he'd given me. Heather was distracted, giggling over the conversation she was having with Roger as he programmed his number into her phone.

"And who's this?" Daryl asked, making his way over to Heather.

"Oh. Hi. I'm Heather!" she said, noticing Daryl for the first time. Daryl raised a thick eyebrow at Roger, then directed his attention back Heather's way.

"Nice to meet you, Heather. And how old are you?"

"Seventeen, why?"

Daryl nodded as he gave Roger a look that basically said, *Get the hell away from her.* Roger, rolling his eyes, told us good night and went back into the club. Heather's face sank into disappointment. She shot me a look of anger, to which I mouthed a silent but exasperated "What?"

"I love this, JT," Daryl said, patting me on the back. "I really do. We usually just get kids from the area or somewhere a little ways north. I think you're our first from Florida in all six years."

I thanked him for the warm welcome and explained what was going on, how we hadn't booked the hotel and didn't have a credit card and were underage. He listened with interest.

"And we have cash, a lot of cash actually, so we'd be happy to pay for somewhere. Like, even if we could crash on your couch, we'd be willing to give you money or something." I tried to hide the desperation but it wasn't very easy. Finally, he smiled knowingly and pulled out his phone.

"Excuse me one second."

He stepped into the alley for his conversation. As Seth and Heather and I eagerly awaited his answer, I checked the stage and saw Lady Rooster was lip-synching masterfully to a medley of anthems that attractive young divas had produced for their gay fans—"Raise Your Fireworks 'Cause You Were Born This Way, Skyscraper."

"Ugh. Why did he scare Roger off?" Heather moaned, slumping against a wrinkled poster advertising something called an underwear party, which seemed pretty self-explanatory.

"Oh, you're on a first-name basis with the bouncer now?" I asked, only slightly more sarcastically than I had intended. Heather shot daggers into me. "That's not creepy to you? Come on. He's like thirty, Heather."

From the stage I heard Lady Rooster ask the crowd if they felt like yet another encore. Clearly, she was enjoying her act a bit more than she let on.

I was dying to see what she'd come up with next. But I was interrupted by Daryl coming back in.

"JT, come here," he said, motioning me over. "Two things. First of all, your friend has no business with Roger. Understand?"

I glanced over my shoulder at Heather, who was grinning as she typed a text on her phone.

"And secondly, it's not much, but some of the drag teens are staying in an apartment over in the East Village. Great kid named Pip—it's his aunt's place. He said the three of you could crash in the living room. I know it's not ideal, but—"

I was so relieved I almost jumped to my feet and threw my arms around him.

Then I remembered: *decorum*. I was a contestant here, even if the judging hadn't formally begun.

But still, I couldn't quite erase the excitement from my voice when I said, "We'll take it!"

Daryl took us over to the East Village apartment where the other queens were letting us crash. The neighborhood was grungier than the area we'd previously been in, which Daryl said was called Chelsea and was apparently, as he put it, "super gay and interesting, once upon a time, before all the rich people came in and ruined it." Daryl was very passionate about his city, even shaking a fist at a brand-new Whole Foods as our taxi drove by it. The entire cab ride over to the apartment, he pointed out numerous places he claimed were once "the real New York." He stopped to mourn an independent video store that had been turned into a frozen yogurt place, claiming that the video store had once been "the heart of all queer punk." He'd lived in the city since he was seventeen, a transplant from Iowa, and from the day he'd arrived he had never lived anywhere else. It was a strange feeling to arrive somewhere so exciting and have someone immediately tell you how much better it used to be. To me, the streets and buildings and people we were passing were the most exciting things I'd ever seen. Even the frozen yogurt place.

I was also really excited by the fact that I was about to meet all these other teenagers who did drag. I was about to go from being the only one around to being surrounded by people I expected to understand why I got such a thrill when I put on a wig. It was like I was about to meet all these people I knew existed in theory but never thought I'd get to meet—my imaginary friends, come to life.

The cab pulled up to a four-story brick building on a quiet side street. Daryl paid the driver and we piled out. The building was nothing special, aside from a rat the size of my mom's dog digging through the trash. It seemed to take a moment to quietly judge us before returning to its digging. Even the rats in this beautiful city were interesting.

"This is the place." Daryl pressed the buzzer, which let out a piercing screech. "I'd say that the buzzer certainly works." The screeching sounded a second time and the door was buzzed open. We went inside and climbed the winding staircase up to the very top floor. I tried desperately not to seem as out of breath as I actually was.

"God! How do the people who live up here not go into cardiac arrest every day?" Heather panted as we reached the top. An apartment door opened and a sleepy-looking Latino boy in a beanie and a T-shirt with the sleeves cut off appeared, revealing a lot of colorful tattooed flowers up and down his super-skinny arms.

"Hey, dude, you Daryl?" He sounded like a mix of Matthew McConaughey and Janice from *The Muppets*.

"Yeah, we spoke on the phone."

"Party, man!" he said, as if the word *party* itself was a response in the way *okay* would be. "I'm Pip!" he said, as if it were a toast.

"Can we . . . come in?" Daryl asked after an awkward pause.

The guy snapped into action. "Oh, sorry. Totally, dudes. And lady—unless that's really convincing drag." While he was a little out of it, he couldn't have been friendlier. He welcomed us into the cramped apartment, the living room seeming to be half the size of the car we'd spent the past three days in. There was enough room for a futon jammed in the corner; it probably took up the entire room when folded out.

Down the hall, which was more like just a wall, there were two doors separated by the bathroom. One of the bedroom doors was shut.

"There's two bedrooms over here, and that's the kitchen." He pointed over to a small corner with a mini-fridge and sink crammed in. "Sorry, I know it's hella small, but it's all good if you want to crash here during the pageant. The world is made for giving, right?"

He finished that by making an unironic peace sign with his hand. Then he went on to explain that he and another contestant from the pageant were crashing in the guest room and that the apartment belonged to his aunt, who owned the place for when she visited the city every once in a while. The rest of the time it sat empty. Pip had come down from Vermont, where he'd been performing in drag off and on since he was six.

I had never met a hippie before but I was pretty sure that was exactly what he was. By which I mean, he talked a lot about the universe and reeked of pot, his eyes so bloodshot it looked like he'd locked himself in a dark room listening to Adele songs on repeat, sobbing, for the previous three days.

These were not what I thought of as *drag qualities*—but then, I also admitted to myself that I had no real idea what *drag qualities* were. YouTube clips and my own feelings were the only two things I had to help me determine this.

"Pip, I appreciate your being so hospitable to your fellow contestants," Daryl said. "You really get what our foundation of building queer community is all about."

"All good, dude. We're all in this crazy thing called life as brothers and sisters. Hey, Tash is sleeping, so if you don't mind keeping it down, that'd be rad." Pip pointed to the closed bedroom door. "Tash just got in from Buffalo. He's really far out. You can stick your stuff wherever, dudes." He winked at Heather. "And lady."

That's when it hit me that all our stuff was still in our car, which was still in the parking garage at the hotel.

"You guys. Our luggage, I completely forgot."

Heather and Seth were just as shocked as I had been.

"Where is it?" Daryl asked. I went on to explain that we'd left the car at the hotel. Daryl rubbed his forehead and said something about how thrilled he was not to have children. I felt bad enough that we'd dragged him out already; I wasn't about to make him go on yet another cab ride with us. We promised him we'd be fine on our own, and, clearly very tired, Daryl said his good-nights, wrote down his number in case we needed anything, and went home.

"Dudes, just take the key with you—that way you don't have to buzz to get back in," Pip offered. Handing Seth the key, he yawned, looking over at the clock on the wall, which read two a.m. "I think I need to crash anyway. You all cool?"

We thanked him again and he brushed it off, saying that it was all about "giving the universe what you hope the universe will give you." Then, as he went to bed, he called out to us, "Night! Party!"

This time *party* took on the meaning of *sweet dreams*, and I found myself even more confused. We went downstairs and got into yet another cab.

A few hours in New York and I was beginning to understand what the whole "city that never sleeps" thing was all about.

"He's nice," Seth said once we were in the dark backseat of the cab. "Pip, I mean." But I could sense a little waver in his voice, a little acknowledgment that he was out of his comfort zone. I was happy to hear it there.

Heather was squeezed between Seth and me, texting like crazy.

"Are you texting that creepy bouncer again?" I asked.

"He's not creepy."

"Heather, you just met him."

"Yeah, and he was very nice to me. Unlike all the gay guys there."

I watched as she sent a kiss emoji.

"What's *that* supposed to mean?"

"Well, you heard that drag queen say they don't normally let girls back there. And the way everyone was staring at me in line. You noticed there wasn't a single girl in sight, right?"

"I'm not sure that lack of competition means that he's a prize," Seth said.

"Plus," I added, "he's too old for you, and Daryl said you should stay away."

"*Of course* he did." Heather scoffed, slapping her phone down into her lap and attempting to cross her arms—no small feat while crammed between Seth and me in the tiny cab.

"I wonder what kind of drag Pip does," Seth wondered aloud.

"I don't know, but I can't imagine what Pip does is anything close to what I'm going to do," I answered. "And I'd say both of us couldn't be more different than Lady Rooster if we made it our life's mission. That's what is cool about drag."

We pulled back up to the fancy hotel and paid the cab driver a small fortune. The same valet attendant in the red vest from earlier opened the cab doors, formally welcoming us to the hotel . . . until he recognized us from earlier and dropped his shtick.

"Oh," he said disdainfully. "You again."

"Good evening." I climbed out of the cab. "We've actually decided to stay somewhere else, so we won't be needing to leave our car here for the night."

The valet attendant rolled his eyes. "Fine. Do you have your ticket?"

After Seth handed over the ticket, the attendant looked at it and pulled our keys out of the little box.

"All right—that'll be three hundred dollars."

I laughed—not to be sarcastic, but because I assumed he was joking around. He *had to be* joking around; we'd only parked the car there three, at most four hours before.

The attendant didn't budge or bat an eye.

"Wait," I said. "You're kidding, right?"

"Why would I be kidding? I don't even like you." The attendant looked at me like I was a guy who'd shown up to the birthday party of one of the most popular kids in school dressed as Maleficent, because he had mistaken the invitation for a costume party but was the only one who did so. Not that this had ever happened to me.

"But three hundred bucks? We were only parked here for a few hours, man," Seth said, using the term *man* to try and toughen up his image. He always did that anytime he needed to impress someone in the service industry.

"Yes, and we only offer overnight parking for our overnight guests. It's the hotel's policy. We charge by the day, not the hour. I wouldn't have parked your car if you hadn't told me you were staying here for the night." He seemed to be taking more pleasure out of all this than seemed necessary. "You're welcome to send a complaint through the Issues and Queries tab on our website. I'll pull your car around. We can take cash or card."

He went through the door marked GARAGE with our keys. I was seething but also too embarrassed to do anything about it. This place already made me feel like a total country bumpkin; at that point all I wanted was to get out of there and back to that crappy apartment of Pip's. At least I felt comfortable in a dump.

"That's so much money, you guys," Heather said the second the attendant was gone. "How much are we going to have left?"

I pulled out the crumpled wad of bills from my pocket.

"Well, with the cabs we've taken, and this three hundred bucks here"—I continued counting—"we have, of this money, one hundred bucks. How much do you guys have left?"

Seth guesstimated he probably had a hundred or so bucks. Heather gritted her teeth into a guilty expression.

"I spent my few bucks on that purse in Ocean City, but I think we can all agree it's extremely cute. Right?" She held up her license plate purse, which couldn't have been less "cute." Now that I knew it'd cost Heather the last of her money, I found it to be full-blown butt-ugly.

The valet honked the horn as he pulled our car around.

"Here you go." He stepped out of the car, leaving it running. "Cash or card, kids?"

It pained my heart as I handed over the three hundred bucks.

"The next time you kids decide to take a sweet little adventure to New York City, maybe stay somewhere a bit more, let's say, your speed. This is a very important hotel and we don't have time to be screwed around."

"Hey! Listen, you dick," Heather shouted as she saw my face shift into utter humiliation. "I'll have you know that you're talking to the future Miss Drag Teen USA!" She patted my shoulder proudly while the attendant rolled his eyes yet again.

"Let's just go," I said under my breath as I buckled my seat belt and began to shut my door. Heather slipped into the back-seat while the attendant stood there, expectantly silent and not moving his gaze.

"Is there something else?" I asked, finally. He sighed and shook his head, then pointed at the sign attached to his valet station: PLEASE TIP.

I dug my hand into my pocket, feeling the remaining few bills of my cash stash with my fingers. Just as I began to disappointedly pull out a bill, Heather rolled down her window.

"Here's a tip, you douchebag!" She hiked her butt up to the open window, pulled down her pants, and mooned him. "Drive, JT!"

Seth and I burst into laughter as we sped away. The laughter continued for a dozen or so blocks . . . which was right when we ran out of gas.

# chapter SIXTEEN

THE ENGINE SPUTTERED AND THE car came to a halt in the middle of the four-lane street. Immediately, a symphony of car horns sounded behind us, with agitated voices shouting at us, in a menagerie of languages, to *get the hell out of the road.*

"You've *got* to be kidding me." I sat very still for a moment. Heather craned her head behind us to assess the late-night mob.

"You guys, there are A LOT of angry New Yorkers behind us" was her conclusion.

The honking and shouting was only getting louder by the second. Seth unbuckled and got out of the car, waving his hands over his head and apologizing to the angry line of traffic. This didn't help; traffic was backing up as cars filled the lanes surrounding us to get by. I had no idea who all these people were and why they were out so late.

"Where are Tina and Bud Travis when you need them, huh?" Seth said as he got back into the car.

A taxi driver navigating his way beside us shouted, "Learn to drive or go back to Florida, idiot!" as Seth shut and locked the door.

"Okay, what the hell are we supposed to do?" I was panicking. "Should we just ditch the car here and tell your parents someone stole it?"

"What?! Are you crazy?!" Seth yelled.

"I'm kidding, doofus."

A police officer on a motorcycle zigzagged his way through the line of cars and up to our window.

"Uh-oh."

He stepped off the motorcycle, leaving its lights flashing, and walked over to the car.

As soon as he got to the window, I launched into my apology. "I'm so sorry, officer. We ran out of gas."

The officer nodded. He had a friendly face, which smoothed over my nerves quite a bit.

"We're from out of town!" Heather shouted from the backseat in an attempt at an explanation.

"The closest gas station is all the way over on Houston; we're going to have to get you kids towed off the road. Can't have you sitting here holding up all these cars." He made a call on his radio, requesting a tow truck. A dispatcher confirmed it was on the way. The officer then stepped into the other lanes and began directing traffic.

"Jesus Christ. This is bad. Why are we having such bad luck?! Is it because we lied to our parents?!" I cried into the dashboard.

I could see that Seth was stressed too, but he was trying to swallow it instead of barfing it up like me. "It's going to be okay," he said. "Just think—all this adversity has got to be a good sign for the pageant."

I knew I should have accepted his comfort. Instead I wanted to smash him in the face.

"In what possible way is this a good sign about *anything*, Seth?" I said, exasperated.

"All great things in life come with setbacks. They only make the eventual success even sweeter. Like when I was walking around my old school, it made me realize how lucky I am that I didn't allow crap that happened to me as a little kid ruin my teenage years. Setbacks are just road signs, ya know?"

I gripped the steering wheel as another angry driver pulled around us, spitting his gum onto our windshield.

"Well, then this pageant better turn out to be real damn sweet."

The tow truck finally arrived and towed the car over to the nearest gas station on Houston. A small part of me still wished they'd somehow lose it. Sure, Seth would have a lot of explaining to do to his parents, but at least we wouldn't be able to leave New York. Also, I was beginning to think the car was somehow cursed.

Begrudgingly, we hopped in yet another cab and followed the tow truck to the gas station, where we filled the gas tank and had to fork over two hundred bucks to the tow service. It was official: In the course of one night, we'd gone from having a lot of money to burn to being unequivocally broke again. I supposed there was a life lesson to be learned in there somewhere, but I was in no mood to learn it.

With our pockets much lighter, we made our way back to Pip's place and found a parking spot nearby. We quietly let ourselves in, hauling all our luggage behind us, and attempted to unfold the creaky old futon without making any noise. We weren't that successful, though, because one of the bedroom doors immediately flew open.

"Who the hell are you?!" a shrill voice screeched, like a parrot that had just learned how to scream. "Don't you dare move, or I'm calling the police! Pip?!"

The body attached to this unfortunate voice stepped out of the shadowy doorway; he was very short, very thin, and very annoyed to have been woken up. He was wearing nothing but a blanket he had wrapped around himself.

"I'm JT," I explained. "Pip said we could crash here. I'm in town for the pageant and we didn't have a hotel, so Daryl suggested we—"

"PIP!" he screeched at the top of his lungs.

Pip's bedroom opened and a very groggy (even groggier than earlier) Pip poked his head out.

"Huh?" Pip rubbed his eyes, his hair looking as if he'd just stepped out of the inside of a cyclone.

"Who the hell are these creatures in my living room?!"

"Tash, it's all good. This is JT and Seth and Heather—they're crashing here for a few days. Daryl brought them over. Guys, this is Tash Sanchez."

Tash was not amused in any way, shape, or form.

"What gives you the authority to allow a group of strangers to barge in here in the middle of the night?! With a female, no less!"

Heather shot me a look that said, *See my point?*

"This is my aunt's apartment," Pip said with a shrug.

Tash, clearly unable to come up with a suitable comeback, simply snarled.

"Hey, listen. We won't be any trouble at all," I assured him. "I'm the only one in the pageant. Seth and Heather are just here for support, so we don't even have a lot of stuff with us."

Tash arched one of his overly plucked eyebrows.

"*You* are in the pageant?"

I nodded as he looked me up and down.

"Oh God." He placed his hand on his heart. "Good luck."

He let out an evil cackle that even on a cartoon witch would have seemed a little too on the nose.

"Hey, don't laugh at him! He's really good!" Heather was pissed. "Wait until you see his talent—he sings like an angel!"

"You sing? Party, dude!" Pip piped in.

Tash scrunched up his face as if concentrating really hard. "You *sing*?"

"Uh-huh."

"Most queens lip-synch."

"Well, he doesn't," Seth challenged.

I could tell Tash was only getting angrier, so I attempted to change the subject.

"Anyway, we're from Florida. Where are you f—"

"Well, whatever it is you do, just understand that some of us take this pageant very, very seriously."

"I take it seriously too."

"This isn't just some little talent show for a boy to put on a dress and sing. If you want to do that, I suggest you go back to Florida and get yourself a job as one of the ugly stepsisters at Disney World."

Tash got a big kick out of this one. I wasn't sure how we'd gotten here, but I realized I had somehow found myself in the midst of a full-blown argument with him.

"Look," I said. "We don't want to cause any trouble, we just need a place to stay, and this appears to be our only option. If it's going to be a big deal, however, we can go somewhere else."

Heather and Seth looked at me with subtle panic in their eyes; they knew just as well as I did that we actually couldn't go somewhere else.

"I think that's a good idea." Tash crossed his arms in victory just as Pip stepped toward me.

"No, dude. You guys stay. Tash, where's your human spirit?"

"Aw, shucks, I guess I left it at the airport. My luggage was over the weight limit as it is," Tash snarked, but Pip didn't budge.

"Well, since this is my aunt's place, and I'm the one renting to *you*, I'm going to put my foot down. JT, Heather, Seth . . . welcome. Tash, deal with it, dude. I've got to get some sleep. Party, y'all."

He went back to his room and shut the door. For a brief moment we were standing across from Tash in a heavily weighted silence.

"Just be careful whose toes you step on, Miss . . . what's your name?"

"JT."

"No, your drag name."

"I don't have one yet."

Tash's mouth dropped open. "You don't have a drag name yet?"

"Not yet. But a friend of mine told me it would find me when the time was right."

Tash stared at me for a moment, then shook his head, cackled again, and shut the door.

Under his breath, Seth murmured, "He seems fun."

My stomach turned as I realized that I'd just had a taste of what a real drag competition was going to be like.

# chapter **SEVENTEEN**

THE NEXT MORNING WAS THE first day of the pageant. I woke up extremely early, due in part to Tash's I'm-*sure*-totally-unplanned decision to sing the entire Mariah Carey song catalog in the shower beginning at seven a.m. I hadn't slept great, seeing as all three of us had been crammed onto the futon like a tube of raw Pillsbury Cinnamon Rolls. I was sleeping in the middle, and around the time that Tash had reached Mariah's "Always Be My Baby" Seth pinched my arm, which was wrapped around him.

"You awake?" he whispered into the sheets.

"What do you think?" Tash had just reached a long belting high note that was almost impressively off-key. Seth laughed.

"How are you feeling?" he asked. I could feel his gross, warm morning breath on my arm but it didn't gross me out because it was him. "About today?"

"Nervous, I guess. But also excited. Yeah, excited."

I still hadn't been able to shake my feelings about Seth's secret and how long it had taken him to open up to me when all that time I thought I was dealing with an open book. I wanted to just let it go, but I simply couldn't. And it wasn't just the secret part. *If he was so good at reinventing himself one time*, a voice inside my head said, *then what's he going to do when he goes off to college and leaves you behind?*

"Hey. You're going to be great, babe. Don't be scared."

"I didn't say I was scared! Don't put words in my mouth—especially weak ones. I have enough to worry about without you piling on." My words came out blunt and weighted. I sounded like a wife who'd stayed silent around her overly critical husband for one too many decades. It was a bit dramatic, especially for this early in the morning, but well, what else was new?

"Okay," Seth said, a little taken aback. "It's going to be a great day."

I wanted that to fix my feelings, but it didn't. I figured the stuff we wanted to fix stuff never fixed stuff; it was the surprises when we were really not expecting them that did. Before I could muster up the nerve to ask Seth why he'd never told me everything about his past, when I'd told him so much, we were interrupted by the sound of chanting from Pip's room, some hippie-dippie-sounding guided meditation. I'd always respected people who could actually meditate and not feel like idiots while they did it. A lot of people pretended to be all Zen and groovy, like our school art teacher, who demanded we call her *Madame* Goldberg. Pip, on the other hand, wasn't putting it on.

"Namaste, dudes and lady!" he announced as he burst out of his room in a floor-length kimono. "Today is the start of a beautiful journey!"

Heather, who had been sleeping, abruptly sat up.

"Is something on fire?" she asked sleepily.

"No, dudes, I'm just burning some sage." Pip held above his head the burning bundle of sage, which was filling the room with smoke and the smell of those expensive candles that don't actually smell *that* good. "This is the perfect chance for us to cleanse our minds before the intense and exciting two days that await us. Are you feeling ready, JT?"

I wasn't sure how to respond. A small, ambitious part of me felt ready, but the main part of me felt completely and totally out of my element.

The bathroom door opened, emitting a cloud of steam into the room. Tash emerged from the fog in a towel, showing off an enormous tattooed rendering of Rihanna across his chest.

"What the hell is that awful smell? Is it one of you?" he shouted, pointing at Heather.

"It's all good, dude. It's just sage. I'm cleansing the energy before we begin the pageant."

"Well, cleanse your own damn energy. That shit smells nasty." Tash slammed his bedroom door as Heather shook her head, staring down at her iPhone.

"You're going to need a lot more than that sage to cleanse the negative energy out of him, Pip," I said.

"Have no fear," Pip advised. "The pageant sees and knows all."


Pip, Tash, and I shared a cab over to the pageant orientation meeting, which was in the lobby of the historic theater in the West Village where the pageant would be taking place. Heather and Seth had wished me luck as they made plans for a day of New York adventuring. I couldn't help but sorta wish I was doing that instead of beginning the next two days of competition.

The lobby was already packed with guys around my age. None of them in drag, but many of them didn't need a wig to display their inner diva. This room was a powder keg of relentless personality and sass.

A circle of chairs was set up in the middle of the room, and as Daryl made his way through the crowd, everyone took a seat and began to quiet down. Or, at least, the noise level was reduced to the *roomful of teenage drag queens* version of quiet, which was more a subtle roar.

"Okay, okay, guys. Let's get started," Daryl projected over the crowd of energetic sass. "Everyone, please have a seat. Welcome! Welcome to the Sixth Annual Miss Drag Teen Pageant orientation." The room cheered. Daryl smiled and waved for everyone to settle down. "As most of you know, I'm Daryl Hart, the executive director of the John Denton Foundation, and I'll be your go-to for any questions or concerns during the next two days. I'm going to pass around a schedule for today and tomorrow." A stack of papers was sent around the circle. "As you'll see, this morning we'll be following our meet and greet with a staging and music rehearsal for this year's opening number. As with every previous year, this opening number is to show the talent each of you inhabit in a group setting, and also for each of you to introduce yourselves to the audience and state something that tells the audience a little about you. Please keep this introduction to a maximum of two sentences. As you can imagine, we've had some past contestants who, let's just say, weren't shy when it came their turn. That did *not* reflect well in their score."

Everyone laughed. I couldn't help but glare over at Tash from the corner of my eye. Luckily he didn't notice.

"After the opening number, we make the very difficult decision of cutting half of you. Which, yes, does mean those people will not get to present their speech or talent."

Everyone moaned.

"I know. I know. But today is a good chance to understand the judging criteria. In fact, later, one of this year's judges will be coming by to tell you what he and his colleagues will be looking for from your 'Why I Drag' speech."

A kid with pink dreadlocks raised his hand.

After being called on, he asked, "Who are the judges this year?"

Daryl smiled proudly. "Well, I am happy to be the first to tell you that along with writer Quentin Brock and Broadway legend Nathan Leary, our esteemed judges from years past, this year we are happy to welcome our newest board member, the *extremely* talented actor Samuel Deckman."

A lot of the guys let out gasps at the name. A small guy who looked like he could have been a ten-year-old girl raised his hand and asked with the deepest voice I'd ever heard, "Is that *the* Samuel Deckman?!"

Daryl smiled and nodded. "Yes. Many of you might know that Mr. Deckman recently came out as a gay man, making him the first gay actor in history to play Aqua Man. In his first public appearance as an out gay man, he'll be helping us select this year's Miss Drag Teen USA!"

Everyone clapped and cheered. Samuel Deckman had recently come out in one of those very public "Yep, I'm Gay" interviews in one of those entertainment magazines that ask newly out celebrities vaguely offensive and incredibly outdated questions like "When did you know?" and "How difficult has it been?" and "Why now?" It was a huge deal he had come out, not just because he was an extremely famous actor but because he was an extremely famous actor who was also extremely attractive.

"At this time, I'd like to turn the floor over to our pageant director and choreographer, Eric Waters, and our musical director, Linda Lambert, who any Broadway fans here will know as the Tony Award–winning writer of *The Lady Isn't Waiting*."

Two adults stood up in the back of the room and made their way up to join Daryl.

"Good morning, guys!" Eric Waters was a handsome, muscular man in his fifties with perfectly coiffed silver hair. He had a very cheery voice. "I'm Eric Waters and this is Linda Lambert." Linda waved. "I've directed and choreographed this pageant since year one. John Denton was a huge inspiration to me when I was around your age; he wrote some of the first gay characters I'd ever read in a book or seen onstage. I couldn't be more excited to continue his legacy with the queer community—and if there's one legacy I think Mr. Denton would've loved the most, it's an original opening number written by a Tony winner, my dear friend Linda Lambert. Not all of you are singers, not all of you are dancers, and I don't expect anyone here to do anything they don't want to do . . . but I think with the talent we've got in this room, we can make this number one of the best we've ever had. How about it? Who in here wants to kick every other year's butt?"

The excitement was infectious. Even *I* was cheering . . . and I hated cheering.

"All right, everybody, follow me to the stage and bring your shoes!"

Pip looked over at me as we headed for the theater.

"Party!"

The opening number was really catchy. They'd only played it a few times and it was already stuck in my head. The first couple of times hearing it we were all crowded around the piano as Linda Lambert sang it along with us, each of us a couple inches taller in the heels we were now wearing. This wasn't a full dress rehearsal, but the director understandably wanted to see if we could make the moves in the proper footwear.

Eric Waters spaced us out onstage into three rows. I was in the middle, directly behind Tash, who absolutely loved that he was blocking me. Pip was somewhere on the other side of the stage and in the back because he was so tall. As with most things, Pip didn't mind this placement one bit.

I was a terrible dancer—I always had been. So the prospect of learning choreography, in heels no less, was very nerve-racking. Eric walked us through the initial steps, which, thankfully, were pretty simple. I was impressed at how easily all twenty guys moved in their heels, including me. Only a handful of people were having a hard time—one particularly unfortunate guy who was even bigger than me couldn't keep his balance to save his life; at one point I really thought he was going to fall off the stage and die. After a while Eric politely suggested he rehearse without the shoes for the time being. I could see the relief all over the guy's face.

*I feel you*, I thought.

The other queens were a smorgasbord of looks and personalities, no two alike. There were skinny boys, heavy boys, black boys, white boys, Asian boys, Latin boys, Indian boys, even an albino boy. I was feeling, surprisingly, at ease. There was something really freeing about being in a group of people so vastly different from one another, and I wondered if that was why New York City itself was so freeing, because it was an entire city made up of vastly different people. It seemed to me that anybody who needed to feel less alienated in life should simply come to New York City for a couple days . . . as long as they steered clear of fancy hotels, valet attendants, and Tash.

I was lost in feeling grateful for having made it all the way there when I realized the music was vamping while Eric Waters repeatedly called my name. I snapped back into reality.

"JT?"

The music stopped.

"Sorry! Sorry!"

"No worries. Like I said, you sashay to the front and land on this green mark, after Milton's turn. You say your introduction, then sashay back to where you are. Got it?"

I nodded, but as I did so, I realized I had forgotten to come up with an introduction line.

"Great, let's try it."

The music started over and Eric called out "Go!" I sashayed up to the green mark, attempting to come up with something in my head, but I had nothing. I hit the mark, the music stopped for my introduction. I stuttered and finally came out with:

"I'm . . . I'm . . . I'm . . ."

I just kept repeating *I'm* as if I were a malfunctioning toy. Finally, Eric called out, "Okay, JT. Just rehearsal. Let's keep moving. Music!"

The music came back and I sashayed, boiling red with embarrassment, back to my spot—only to discover it wasn't even my spot.

I was going to have to find my place—and soon.


After we locked down the choreography, we took a ten-minute break and drew numbers for the pageant order. I drew twelve. I was trying my hardest to put on a brave face around these people; if I'd learned one thing from watching more reality television than should be humanly possible, it was that competitors thrived off one another's fear.

"Hey, you! What's your number?"

I turned to see the short guy with the deep voice. He was rail thin, with beautiful wavy hair. He stood with both hands on his hips and wore a skintight T-shirt with a picture of a unicorn on it.

"Twelve," I told him. I held out the piece of paper I'd just drawn, which caused the boy to whistle over to a very handsome and much larger guy on the other side of the stage.

"Red! Get over here! I found twelve. I'm Milton, by the way."

Red came bumbling over. He was a giant—six foot six at the very least, with bigger muscles than anyone on my school's football team. However, when he spoke, his voice was higher than anyone on my school's cheerleader squad. He was like a one-stop pep rally.

"Hi, I'm Charlie," he said, offering his hand. I shook it at my own risk. "Call me Red, though, because I hate the name Charlie and I look great in red. You'll see later. Anyway, listen. I'm number thirteen. Any chance you'd switch with me?"

Milton leaned forward. "Red's been terribly superstitious ever since he stepped on a crack and actually broke his mother's back. Long story, but it wasn't pretty."

I looked down at the thirteen on his paper. "So you want me to have the unlucky number?"

Red scrunched up his face, clearly a little embarrassed to be asking such a blatantly sabotaging favor. But before he could apologize, Tash appeared beside me.

"Yeah," he clucked. "That's *exactly* what he's asking. You superstitious too?"

Tash managed to carry a dark cloud over him at all times. No matter the conversation he entered, you felt the wave of bad attitude cover it immediately.

"Hi. Guys, this is Tash."

Milton and Red looked at each other apprehensively, crossing their arms.

"Oh. We know," Milton said.

The two shot Tash a suspicious look while Tash simply rolled his eyes.

"Didn't realize I'd be seeing you two here."

"It's nice to see you too, Tash," Milton said. For his part, Red seemed to cower in fear behind his tiny friend. "You remember Red, don't you?"

Tash pursed his lips and nodded.

"I haven't seen you since, what? Miss Teen Atlantic City?" Milton awkwardly proceeded. "How've you been?"

"Fine." Tash's answer had all the feeling of a dial tone.

"Oh. You two know each other?" I asked, sensing the kind of tension reserved for gang fights.

"We do." Milton's once-perky voice had grown icy cold.

"We met doing Miss Teen New Jersey together. I won," Tash hissed. "By a landslide."

"And then I beat him in Miss Teen Atlantic City. *Also* by a landslide." Milton ignored Tash's eyes burning into the side of his face.

"Wow. I didn't realize there were so many drag teen pageants." I was hoping to break the tension, but it didn't work. Milton clearly had a lot to say about and to Tash, but he kept quiet and polite, with a towering yet fearful Red behind him. The two of them passively turned their backs to Tash and talked only to me.

"So, JT. Are you a glamour queen or a comedy queen?"

"Huh?"

Tash laughed as he pushed me aside to get back into the conversation. "He's neither; this one doesn't even have a drag name!"

Red, having had enough, stepped forward, towering over Tash.

"You know what, Tash? Why don't you go find somebody who isn't already tired of your mean-girl routine to talk to? We're all good without it here."

Tash, fuming, shot back, "It's not a routine. I *am* a mean girl." Then he stormed off as Milton subtly mouthed his thanks to Red.

"Be careful of that one, gurl," Milton said as soon as Tash was out of sight.

"Why?" I asked.

Milton and Red looked at each other with the weight of an enormous secret behind their eyes.

"She's bad news," Red said nervously, looking over to Milton for permission to continue. Milton nodded to go ahead. "She didn't used to be. A while ago, she and Milton were super close."

"The closest," Milton interjected. "Until. Well . . ." He looked to Red to continue.

"Until Milton won Miss Teen Atlantic City. That's when Tash turned against him. See, Tash had never lost before."

"Like, ever!" Milton interjected again.

"And she makes a good queen, too."

"Really good!" Milton couldn't stop chiming in. "So good that she doesn't even have a last name, she just goes by *Natasha*, like she's Madonna or Meryl or something."

"So now she does whatever it takes to keep anyone from getting in between her and the crown. And I mean anything." There was a trace of something sinister in Red's voice. "She's not even here for the scholarship—Tash doesn't want to go to college. Her ten-year plan is to win *Drag Race* and join *The View* as its first drag co-host. And honestly? I bet she could."

"But what do you mean? When you say she'll do *anything*, what does that include?"

Milton and Red looked at each other with fear in their eyes, like people in a scary movie telling somebody what happened that terribly fated night. They even checked over their shoulders to make sure no one was listening in.

"I heard she poisoned Snow Cone Joan in the Buffalo pageant with some expired cottage cheese at the continental breakfast so she'd be too sick to compete," Red whispered.

"And I heard that she convinced the judges that Trixie Treat was actually twenty-two to get her disqualified, and you don't even want to know what she allegedly did to Nicole Just-Kidding-Man," Milton murmured.

"She. Stole. Her. Wig." Red shuddered as he said this.

I gasped. I didn't even want to tell these two that I had not only made an enemy out of Tash but that we were currently sleeping under the same roof.

"Anyways," Red chirped. "Glamour queen or comedy queen? You *must* understand the difference. Milton? Explain to our new friend."

Milton straightened his shoulders and stepped forward like someone with perfect grades in a spelling bee.

"A glamour queen is a queen whose tastes are for decadence, beauty, and class. A glamour queen puts her elegant look above

all else. Your classic pageant queen. Red is a glamour queen."
Red smiled. "A comedy queen, while still glamorous—because
after all, gurl, this is still drag—is a queen who uses humor to
sell her glamour and style. A comedy queen might not have the
prettiest gown, but she'll always leave you laughing."

"Milton is a comedy queen," Red added.

I stood there processing all this new information, a little
overwhelmed. Milton and Red could tell.

"Hey, don't panic," Red said. "Drag isn't just about labels
like that—you can be whatever you want. Sorry. You new at
this or something?"

I wasn't sure whether to admit to these two that this was
only my second time, but for some reason I trusted them. Besides,
even if I couldn't be a glamour queen or comedy queen, at the
very least I could be an honest queen.

"This is my second time."

"Ever?" Milton asked in shock.

"Uh-huh." I could feel my cheeks getting redder, which was
weird, since I was talking to someone named Red. "Please don't
tell anybody. I know most everyone here is a pro at this but,
well, I love doing it and I desperately need the scholarship and I
don't want people to think I'm disrespectful to the drag world
by just doing it again for a scholarship because that's not the
only reason, it's just a big one. I really *want* to be great at this
because it brings me a lot of joy, like the most joy I've ever felt
doing something. And I hope by doing it I can figure out how to
be who I'm supposed to be. I want to love myself, and when I'm
in drag I think I actually might."

Milton and Red smiled at me. I could see something dancing around in both their eyes.

"Gurl, you just found your introduction."

They both hugged me, and in our embrace, I saw Tash watching from the wings, hating every second of it.

# chapter **eighteen**

NATHAN LEARY ARRIVED AFTER LUNCH. He was one of those actors who had been around since I could remember. He was never a big movie star, but he was always the type of actor who popped up in everything from sitcoms to historical dramas about obscure but irrationally funny Founding Fathers. Meanwhile, Broadway was his main home. He was probably around seventy years old, so he had stories on just about every important celebrity there'd ever been in the past fifty years; if he hadn't starred with them on some TV movie or Broadway show, he'd probably played their sassy assistant in a major (or not so major) movie . . . or at least he'd have a story that claimed so. He'd been openly gay since long before being openly gay made you cool, and I thought he was forgotten for that sometimes. Sometimes it felt like the celebrities who were out before out was cool were not considered as cool as those celebrities who'd only recently come out after being prodded to do so. People always loved something new and shiny, I guessed. Nathan Leary, however, was the real deal.

He was there to give us the talk about what the judges would look for in our "Why I Drag" speeches. A natural performer, it seemed he was taking this opportunity to workshop a full one-man show for this room of eager gay queen-teens. Who could blame him?

"*Why I drag.* Think about that statement for a second, boys. Think about it." Leary projected to the back of the theater even when he wasn't in a theater. "Why do I drag?"

He looked around the roomful of guys my age who had also, undoubtedly, grown up with his performance as a beloved drag queen in the cult hit movie *Has Anybody Seen Mrs. Mapplethorpe?*

"That's what we want—we want you to dig deep inside yourself and tell us *why*. We don't want some stock pageant answer—that's not what this is about. This is about *you*. What's in your heart. Do all of you understand that?"

The room let out a moderately enthusiastic yes as Leary launched into a long story about the first time he'd worked with a long-dead Broadway legend named Mary Martin and how that taught him to speak only from the heart, and to never eat mayonnaise right before curtain. Which said a bit more about Mary Martin than I cared to know. The truth was, I sorta knew "why I drag," but I wasn't so sure I'd be able to explain all that eloquently onstage.

"Now, speaking of my time working with Mary Martin—Daryl wants me to remind you that after this, you'll each do a walk-through of your talent segment. If anyone needs an accompanist, we ask that you sign up here."

Nathan passed around a clipboard as everyone applauded his speech. I'm not sure any of us were particularly moved by what he'd said—but he was a judge, and judges, we knew, love their applause as much as the next person. Especially when they're actors.

Now was my time to freak out about the talent portion of the competition. I'd decided to sing—because my only other option was a demonstration on how to most effectively pump gas. But Tash's condescension at the notion of singing—and Lady Rooster's triumph without singing a note—made me wonder if I wasn't making a big, big mistake.

Only a handful of contestants had signed up for an accompanist, which meant that most people were planning to lip-synch. And a few people were using the accompanist for background music in various physical talent bits, like Red, or number four, Miss Hedini, this guy with the biggest Afro I'd ever seen, who was doing a highly elaborate magic routine where he chopped a go-go boy in half. I'd never even seen a go-go boy, let alone one cut in half. Along with me, the only other two people singing were number eighteen and nineteen, who had defied pageant history by getting the judges to agree to allow them to perform a duet ("Defying Gravity" from *Wicked*, with number nineteen literally lifting into the air at the end using a small trampoline hidden underneath a floor-length witch's costume).

Then there was me, unlucky number thirteen.

"Hi. Linda Lambert. But you can call me Linda." She shook my hand as she stood up from the piano. She had a super-friendly face and supportive smile, and spoke with the prettiest British accent I'd ever heard that wasn't from Helen Mirren in a moderately boring movie. "You're number thirteen? What am I playing?"

"Yeah. I'm JT. It's really nice to meet you. I'm a big Broadway nerd, and I went to see the tour of your show twice when it came to Tampa, so it's crazy that you're going to be the one playing for me. I'm going to sing."

"You're so sweet! Also, I'm glad somebody's actually singing." She lowered her voice. It was so exciting to be sharing a secret with a Tony Award winner! "Just between you and me, I think it's a real waste of talent that we've got this roomful of teenage divas and they're all lip-synching to somebody else's voice. Know what I mean?"

I told her I did, but that I'd deny it if she repeated I'd said so. She got a big kick out of that.

"Got your sheet music?"

I opened up my backpack and reached inside for the "Part of Your World" pages. As I did, I noticed the autographed sheet music from Tina Travis and her "People Care" song. I paused, my hand staying still inside the bag. I knew "Part of Your World" by heart. (I mean, who doesn't?) But I had an idea and my gut was saying to go for it. My experience with Tina Travis was one of the coolest things that had ever happened to me, and singing the song itself actually meant something to me now, as opposed to "Part of Your World," which meant something to me when I was six and still thought it was relatable to yearn to have legs.

"You okay? Something got your hand in there?" Linda asked with a bemused grin as I stood there with my hand bizarrely stuck inside my bag.

"Sorry! I just . . ." I knew I had to decide, and finally I just thought *screw it* and pulled out Tina's music and handed it to Linda.

"Tina Travis? Wow. I haven't seen her name in a long time." Linda laughed. "Where did you even get this?"

I didn't want to seem like some snobby kid who knew famous people, mainly because I wasn't some snobby kid who knew famous people—I'd just happened to have one help me with a flat tire a few days ago.

"Oh, just found it at a yard sale. My mom always played her songs when I was growing up."

Linda smiled as she placed the music on the piano. "That's lovely. Shall we?"

She began playing and I began sweating. Everyone in the room was waiting. I couldn't believe I was about to do what I was about to do, but I had no choice. It was too late now to go back, so I went forward. She kept playing, supportively chiming in every once in a while to tell me to slow it down or speed it up. At one point I heard someone across the room audibly wonder, "What the hell is this song anyway?" and I felt proud—proud of myself and proud of my friend Tina Travis, a great icon who'd been lost by time.

By the midsection of the song, everyone in the room had stopped what they were doing to stare at me. I couldn't tell if this was a good thing or bad thing, but I didn't let myself freak out. I kept picturing Tina's face in my head, telling me I could do it, and somehow that worked.

As the song ended and the room was quiet for a brief second, Linda looked up at me and mouthed "Awesome" while a handful of people in the room clapped politely. I couldn't believe it, but I had just performed in front of a roomful of strangers and I didn't even feel like crawling into a cave and dying. In fact, I was feeling readier and more capable of doing this pageant than ever before. Maybe I was out of my mind, but I really could feel it—I was close enough to being Miss Drag Teen USA to almost reach out and touch it. I'd never felt confident about anything in my life, and suddenly, there it was, this strange and foreign feeling of confidence. I didn't even know what to do with it. That's when I realized I'd found the second thing on my to-do list: I *did* have a talent, I just had to ignore my own bullshit long enough to do it. I pulled out the list and, with a pencil lying on the piano, crossed out number two.

Two down, two more to go.

# chapter NINETEEN

I WAS ON CLOUD NINE when I met up with Heather and Seth after rehearsal at the cutest New York café around the corner, which I realized once I walked inside was actually just a Starbucks. They'd had their own kind of New York sightseeing-packed day, taking selfies in front of Carrie Bradshaw's brownstone and walking around Central Park for, as an exhausted Heather put it, "what felt like three and a half days." The evening's plan was to go out for a big and cheap-as-possible dinner in Little Italy. Then I had to go back to the apartment to write my "Why I Drag" speech.

"It was crazy," I told them. "I wish you two could have been there. I was standing at the piano and something in my head told me to do Tina's song instead of 'Part of Your World.' And I did it, and I was terrified, but when I finished, people clapped. It felt so good, you guys!" I couldn't stop smiling.

"Babe, that's amazing. I'm so proud of you." Seth kissed my forehead, getting crumbs from the black-and-white cookie he was eating in my hair. "So you're feeling ready for tomorrow?"

"I feel scared to say so." I looked around, as if one of the other contestants might be listening. "But yeah, I actually am. Is that cocky bad luck?"

"NO! Don't be ridiculous!" Heather slapped the table. "You *should* feel ready! You're going to kick drag ass!"

We walked all the way down to Little Italy, subtly using the maps on our phones to try to look like we knew where we were going. For some reason, looking like a tourist in New York seemed like the most mortifying thing any of us could ever do. I supposed when you wanted to belong somewhere as badly as all three of us wanted to belong here, you hoped people would just assume you already did.

Seth was a natural at it, which didn't surprise me at all. I wondered if he felt like he was already walking through his future. I wondered if he felt me by his side while he did.

Little Italy wasn't quite as magical as it seemed in movies. The coolest part was the Little Italy sign made out of lights that hung from the streetlamps. It was so crowded, and everywhere we went, so many people shoved menus in our faces that we didn't really have a chance to make up our own minds or actually look around. We finally settled on a place midway down the block because we were tired of all the pushy people with the menus and because it had our one requirement: red-and-white Italian restaurant tablecloths. Heather and Seth were immediately excited because the waiter didn't card them; they shared a carafe of red wine that smelled like expired salad dressing.

"Can you believe we're really here?" Heather asked, already tipsy on her second glass of the nasty wine. "We're *so Girls* right now!"

"You guys, I'd like to make a toast." I lifted up my Diet Coke. "I can't thank you enough for doing this with me. I can't believe I'm lucky enough to have such amazing friends, and I just want you to know I wouldn't be here without you."

Heather lifted her glass, spilling a little bit onto the table. "Oh, JT, don't worry. We know."

Seth remained strangely silent, but he did clink my glass, at least.

I spent the rest of the dinner gossiping about all the other contestants in the pageant. I told them about how everyone seemed to be terrified of pissing off Tash, and speculated about whether Red and Milton were a couple, and detailed the Afro guy's magic act. I told them about this contestant named Roxanne Roll, who absolutely terrified me because she seemed to have made it her mission to be terrifying and, as she had referred to it to Eric Waters, *hard-core*.

I waited until the end to mention that the guest judge was going to be Sam Deckman.

"SAM DECKMAN?!" Heather shouted, her jaw almost dropping into our basket of garlic knots.

"Shhhh. But yes. Apparently he's on their board of directors. They've also got Nathan Leary and—"

"Do I get to meet him? I want to meet him. I have to, JT. It's only fair. You know how much I loved *Aqua Man*!" Heather managed to say all of this in one breath.

"I'll see what I can do. But you have to promise you won't embarrass me."

"What's that supposed to mean?" she asked, offended.

"You can come on a little strong when you're excited. You know that. Look at how you acted around that creepy bouncer at that club. Plus, right now you have an enormous glob of garlic-and-olive-oil sauce on your chin."

"He has a point, Heather," Seth added.

I could tell we had both said the wrong thing and, frankly, replaying the words inside my head, they sounded pretty bitchy. *Oh God*, I thought, *is Tash rubbing off on me?*

"Sorry! That came out wrong. Forget it. Also, you really do have pasta sauce all over your face."

She grabbed a napkin, humiliated. My instinct was to keep apologizing, but I could tell Heather's guard was up from the way she kept staring at her phone for the rest of the meal.

"So are you ignoring us now?" I asked carefully. Heather looked up, as if she hadn't heard me.

"Huh?"

"Okay, so you are."

She slapped her phone down onto the checkered tabletop.

"You can be such a jerk sometimes."

"I was just messing around," I argued.

"You think I'm here to be your sidekick. The fat girl who devotes her life to her two gay friends."

The way she said it, it sounded like something she had clearly been thinking about for a while now. I had never thought of Heather as anything other than my best friend, ever. Best friend was not a sidekick position.

"No. That's not it at all."

"I want some adventure too. Or is that too much to ask because I'm the third wheel? The girl?"

"Hey," Seth intervened, "don't say that. JT was trying to protect you. That guy *is* a creepy bouncer."

"I do *not* need protecting," she said loudly, almost at a yell, then went back to her phone.

"Let's just drop it," I said. But even though we dropped it, it stayed with us for the rest of the meal. I knew it was pretty bad because none of us wanted dessert. Not even as we passed at least a half-dozen ice-cream places on our way back to the apartment.

Heather held back, texting some more. This gave me a little space to ask Seth how he was doing.

"What do you mean?" he asked.

"I mean, how are you doing?"

"I'm good. It's great here."

"You had a great day?"

"Totally."

I felt like a fool for wanting to ask, *But didn't you miss me?* I'd said I'd missed him, hadn't I? Why isn't it possible to just hold up a sign that says exactly how you're feeling without having to say it?


Both Tash and Pip were out of the apartment when we got there, Pip having signed up for a three-hour group chant around the corner to get himself into the right headspace for the pageant. I had no idea of or interest in where Tash might be; I was mostly just happy to have the place to ourselves, free of his gloomy cloud of bitchiness.

"Where is my blue suitcase?" I asked, eyeing three pieces of luggage in the corner of the room where once there had been four.

"I put them all over there when we brought them in." Seth pointed to the three suitcases.

"Yes, but one is missing."

"It is?"

"Are you guys messing with me?"

Seth and Heather exchanged confused expressions as I began ripping through the other bags, opening and dumping out the contents of each, hoping maybe we'd double packed or something. There had to have been a mistake, a terrible mistake! Seth joined me in my search, looking under the futon, in the bathroom, everywhere, to no avail. Heather, still pissed off from dinner, was actively zero help.

"Maybe they're in the car. Maybe I left them in there last night."

"But we brought all the bags inside last night," Seth reminded me calmly. My eyes shot daggers at him until he quietly backed away and went to search in the foyer.

I let myself into Pip's room to make sure the costumes hadn't been put there by mistake.

Pip's room was way more orderly than I would have expected. His costumes hung in garment bags in the open closet, while everything else had a clearly designated spot. Mind you, the bulk of his belongings were a row of wigs on Styrofoam heads, a stack of incense sticks, some weird-looking prayer beads, a comically enormous bong, and a framed photograph of Deepak Chopra standing next to Angelina Jolie and Elmo. My costumes were nowhere in sight, and it was clear Pip never could have mixed them up with his own.

"Not in the kitchen or the hallway," Seth said, with a nervous look of defeat.

The search was pointless. I knew exactly what had happened—I could feel it in my gut. I was almost afraid to say it out loud because it would only confirm what I was fearing. From the minute he laid eyes on me, for whatever bizarre reason, Tash had clearly decided I was enemy number one, and today's rehearsal had clearly been the final nail in my coffin. I was on the verge of tears.

Seth saw this, and wanted to head it off. "Wait. Let's calm down. Panicking or crying is not going to solve anything." He started pacing the tiny space around the futon. "Let's think."

"It was Tash," I spat out quickly, as if the words themselves tasted gross in my mouth.

"Huh?"

"He hates me. You've seen the way he looks at me when I talk about the pageant."

Seth sighed. "Come on, JT. Don't be so insecure. Nobody would go out of their way to sabotage you like that."

You know how sometimes people say just the exact wrong thing and everything suddenly goes into slow motion as you lose your shit? So yeah, that happened.

"Well, excuse me, Seth. Not all of us can be secure as you, Mr. Perfect."

"Hey, JT. Come on. That's not fair. I told you I don't like when you call me perfect."

"I've told you everything, ever since I've known you. I've shared everything and you acted so open and honest, but all that time you had this past you never told me about. Why? Because you didn't trust me to hold your baggage but just wanted to hold on to mine. Did it feel good to be the stable one for the crazy mess? And is it possible, just a little bit possible, that now that I'm getting my life together, now that I'm actually excited about something, you don't know what the hell to do except tell me how insecure I'm being? Because that's the guy you signed up for?"

"JT. Hey, come on."

"I have trusted you with *so much*, Seth. Everything I feel, I tell you. Because I love you. And this enormous thing, this person you used to be—you never thought to tell me? It hurts my feelings, okay? It hurts my stupid feelings."

I stormed into the bathroom, flinging open the door to find Heather midway into putting on more makeup than I'd ever seen someone wear—and lest we forget, I had spent the day with drag queens. She'd crammed herself into the kind of tight black dress she *never* would have worn in Florida. In fact, it was the kind of tight black dress that very well might have been illegal in some parts of Florida. She looked up at me, guilty but assured. Then she brushed past me and Seth, eyes glued to her phone, where she was mid-text, grabbed her purse, and was out the door.

Seth and I looked at each other, knowing exactly what was going on—but not having any way to stop it.

"I'll see if I can catch her," Seth said, running out the door. I wondered if he was just taking it as a convenient excuse to leave, escaping my characteristically random freak-out.

"I can't believe this!" I screamed.

But there was no one around to hear me.

# chapter TWENTY

SETH CAME BACK A FEW minutes later, shaking his head.

"Go work on your speech," he said. Code words for *I don't really want to talk to you right now.*

I tried. For hours, I tried. Seth was right next to me, not prodding me at all. It felt weird to not be prodded.

It was after midnight when Pip got home, coming in with a sweaty yoga mat and a disgusting-looking green juice. I was comatose on the futon, in a state of shock and defeat. At this point, I figured why bother writing a speech if I had no costume to deliver it in.

"Salutations, dudes. I didn't expect you both to still be awake," Pip announced, predictably cheery.

I launched into the whole story about the costumes and how we suspected Tash. I asked him a million questions without giving him a chance to answer any of them: "Did you see the costumes?" "Did Tash say anything about taking them?" "Has Tash ever stolen before?" "Is Tash some kind of comic book villain?"

Pip was a little overwhelmed by all my questioning, which was understandable seeing as he'd just come from a group chant and meditation and had now just walked into a frenzy of crazed paranoia. He attempted to calm me down, but Seth told him that, based on personal experience, it was probably not the best idea to try to calm me in the midst of panic and that he should probably just go to bed. Pip told me he'd pray for the almighty universe's rightful return of the costumes, and I tried my hardest not to scream again.

It was getting later and later, but I couldn't go to sleep until I spoke to Tash or Heather. She wasn't responding to our calls or our texts. It wasn't that out of character for Heather to run off in the midst of being upset, but this was New York City; this was different. I knew Heather wouldn't do anything to put herself in immense danger, but she was definitely capable of doing something stupid, like putting on a skimpy dress and meeting up with a thirty-year-old bouncer from a gay nightclub who she'd met only once before.

I stopped calling and texting her over and over, as I figured that was only making things worse. She was tired of feeling babied by us, she wanted her own adventure, and after dragging her across the country, who was I to deny her that?

Seth dozed off beside me on the futon. I lay wide-awake, waiting for the moment when the front door finally burst open and Tash stomped into the room.

"Sorry!" he said loudly. "Hope I didn't wake you up! I know it's important to get a lot of rest before the pageant."

I stood up, trying my hardest to maintain composure.

"Tash. I know what you did and it's not okay."

Tash sheepishly held up a grocery bag with a carton of ice cream in it.

"I know, I know. I have *no* business having ice cream the night before a pageant, but I just couldn't resist. Fine, twist my arm, I'll share. Shall I get us some spoons? Where's your little girlfriend?"

I could feel the beads of sweat forming on the back of my neck, the ones that always came when I had to deal with confrontation of any kind.

"I'm talking about my costumes."

Tash's face shifted into the kind of phony expression you'd make in a school play when the teacher asked you to look *surprised*.

"Don't you dare pretend you don't know what I'm talking about, Tash! Don't you dare!"

I was about to lunge in his direction, but Seth, awake now, put his hand around my waist.

"Okay, babe," he soothed. "Don't lose your cool."

Tash clucked his tongue. "I have no idea what it is you're accusing me of right now, but I have to say, I find it utterly offensive. You know what? For that, I'm not going to share my ice cream with you."

Tash made his way to his room, but before he shut his door, he stopped and, with the cruelest of smiles, said, "And, Miss Thing, I saw those costumes, and whoever *did* steal them probably did you a very big favor."

He slammed his door and locked it before I had a chance to explode. I was trembling; I had never experienced something so blatantly cruel in my life. Before I knew it, tears were streaming down my face. Seth pulled me into his chest. I could hear his heart beating as I choked on my cries.

It felt stupid to cry about a polyester pantsuit and some gowns, but that's exactly what I was doing.

And wigs. I was also crying over the wigs.


All night, I tossed and turned with the images of my missing marabou circling my mind. Also, Heather hadn't come home.

Seth was keeping some distance, but not so much that he made me feel like I was in this alone. I really appreciated that. Every now and then he'd wake up and murmur something like, "We've come so far already" or "We'll figure something out." Then he went back to sleep, and I could only hope the perfect solution would come to him in a dream. Because right now the pageant was less than twenty-four hours away, and I had zero costumes and zero wigs.


When it was time to go in the morning, Pip offered to walk over with me. Tash's door was still closed—there was no way to storm his room and get to rehearsal on time. Seth told me not to worry about Heather, that he'd track her down and make sure everything was okay. I told him that I'd stop worrying about it, but it was clear that neither of us believed it.

That morning's rehearsal was spent running through the

choreography for the opening number. When Tash got there, he avoided any form of eye contact with me whatsoever, and I was too tired to keep arguing anyway. Eric Waters was in drill-sergeant mode, shouting at us from the back of the theater.

"How was your night? Did you get into any trouble? We did!" Milton bounced over and asked in one single breath, while we were on break.

He and Red shared excited smiles as they recounted their outrageous New York night, which included seeing a musical about Diana Ross ("The wigs, gurl! The wigs were to die for!") and dinner at some fancy restaurant in the West Village where they were pretty sure the person seated behind them was one of the ladies who had been a Real Housewife of somewhere, at some point, maybe. They were buzzing with delight and it was hard not to envy them.

"What about you?" Milton asked, this time pausing for my response.

"I . . . well, I had dinner and then, um, it wasn't that great." I fumbled all over my words and blushed. Was I actually going to cry *here* over lost wigs?

"Did something bad happen?"

My attempt to keep it bottled up was clearly not working, I could feel my hysteria creeping out of me like coffee spilling out of a Starbucks cup when they overfill it and then have the audacity to still put on the lid so that it becomes your problem and not theirs once you walk out of the store.

"My costumes, my wigs . . . all of it . . . He took them."

"Who did?!"

I lowered my voice, taking deep breaths to calm myself down. "Tash. I think. He says he didn't, but they were at the apartment and I know Pip didn't take them. And you said that he took that one queen's wig a while back, right? I don't know what to do. I want to tell Daryl or somebody, but I'm afraid they won't believe me and will think that I'm only after their sympathy."

Red and Milton had become very serious, listening like detectives at a brutal crime scene.

"Don't! Don't tell *anyone*." Milton was eerily calm but stern. "He will find a way to turn it against you."

A paranoid Red kept looking over his shoulder and shushing us to keep it down. Milton obliged, visibly shaken.

"The last time somebody turned Tash in for stealing a wig, he framed the person for stealing *his*. That was poor Miss Tootsie Roll, and she was never the same after she got disqualified from the pageant. Poor thing, she works at an Old Navy in White Plains nowadays."

Milton winced at his own words.

"Disqualified?" I asked. "But how did Tash get away with it?!"

Milton shook his head with a frown. "I don't know, girl. But he did, and he will again. Trust me. He always gets away with his shenanigans. The only thing you can do is ignore them and bounce back."

"But I don't have other wigs, or costumes, and I'm assuming no one here has extras, right?"

Milton and Red told me how much they wished they could help but that they only packed what they needed. They tried to calm me down, telling me that it would work out as long as I didn't say a word.

I was called to the stage to rehearse my number, which was the last thing I wanted to be doing. Linda Lambert played Tina's song and I sang it as best I could, but there was nothing there, none of the emotion or notes that had been there before. I was just trying to get it over with. When I'd finished, Linda looked at me quizzically.

"That was . . . good." She tried to make her lie sound convincing, but it didn't work. "Are you okay?"

I could feel everything welling up inside me, and I wanted to tell her what had happened. I felt like I could trust her—that maybe, hell, she'd loan me one of *her* pantsuits. But standing in the wings directly behind her were Milton and Red, both mouthing for me not to say a word.

"I'm fine. Just a little tired."

"No problem. I get it. Save your energy for tonight. After yesterday's rehearsal, I'm certain you've got your song down perfectly. Just do it like you did then and they'll go crazy for you."

Linda's Tony Award–winning supporting words would've meant a lot more if I wasn't wondering if I'd get to perform in the pageant at all.

✳   ✳   ✳

I was sitting in the dressing room with headphones, not actually listening to anything but wearing them just so that no one would try and talk to me. My phone lit up with a text message from Seth reading: *Come outside when you can. I have something to show you.*

I snuck out the stage door into the alley behind the building. Seth was there with an enormous plastic shopping bag.

"Ta-da!" Seth exclaimed, handing over the bag. Inside was a pile of multicolored clothes and one super-cheap-looking pink wig.

"What is all this?" I asked.

"I know it's nowhere near as nice as the stuff you lost, but it's better than nothing."

I pulled the wig out of the bag. It was one of those awful bright-colored bob wigs you buy at the drugstore during Halloween that are marked 100% FLAMMABLE MATERIALS.

If I kept going like this, that would end up being my drag name.

"Wow. Thanks." I attempted to sound sincere, but with the sad excuse for hair in my hand, it wasn't easy.

"Hey. You don't have to pretend to like it. I know it sucks, but it was sorta the best I could afford."

If I could have stepped outside my body in that moment, I might have seen just how lucky I was, with or without this pageant. However, stepping outside your body is impossible, and I was a moderately troubled seventeen-year-old boy freaking out about his missing wigs. This was not a time for introspection.

"JT, look. I'm not going to tell you not to worry. I can see how that's not what you need right now. I get it. But while you're worrying, let's try to focus on what you still have. Because this contest isn't about the outfit or the wig—it's about you being the best drag teen you can be. And I have *no idea* what that means, but I know that you do, and that's what will get you through. "

I understood his point and he was absolutely right. The only problem was that to be the best drag teen I could be, I needed to actually *be* in drag.

"Where's Heather?" I asked.

Seth sighed. "She was just getting in when I left this morning."

"Was she okay?"

"I don't know. She went straight to the bathroom and told me she was fine, that she'd had a good time, and that she'd see me later. I refused to leave for a while, wanting the full story, but she told me she wasn't going to budge until I'd left her alone. So I left her alone. At least temporarily."

"Is she still coming tonight?"

"Absolutely. She even said so before I left. Speaking of which—how'd your speech turn out?" Seth asked, pulling me out of my thoughts as he shoved the wig back into the plastic shopping bag. I stopped dead in my tracks. My speech. Crap times one million. With everything that had happened the night before, I had forgotten to write my speech. An entire three-to-five-minute speech that I had to perform in less than five hours and I still hadn't written a single word. It felt like forgetting a math quiz, only worse, because I actually cared about this.

From my panicked expression, Seth knew exactly what had happened.

Before I could say anything, the stage door squeaked open and Miss Hedini, the drag-queen magician, poked her head out.

"Hey. You're JT, aren't you? Daryl's got to approve everybody's costumes. Hurry in here!"

The door shut behind him as Seth handed me the shopping bag.

"I am doomed," I said.


Inside the dressing room, everyone had their outfits on display for Daryl and his assistant. He was going through the wardrobe to make sure everyone would be dressed within the guidelines of the pageant. I walked in as he was saying no to a few different looks for being too suggestive or risqué. I felt my stomach turn as I stared down at my plastic shopping bag.

The gowns these guys had were amazing, like the kind of thing Jennifer Lawrence would wear to the Oscars or, in some cases, the kind of thing Lady Gaga would wear to the grocery store. Their wigs were also perfect, the kind of expensive-looking wigs Tina had given me. At the other end of the long, narrow dressing room, I could see Tash nonchalantly combing one of her three stunning lace-front wigs that I reckoned were all actual human hair.

I waited with dread as Daryl and his assistant made their

way over to my side of the dressing room. Daryl was gushing all over the outfits held by the guy next to me, the only contestant with facial hair, who'd introduced himself, aptly, as Katy Hairy.

I awaited my execution.

After he'd finished praising Katy, Daryl stood before me. "Hello there, JT. Great seeing you."

As he smiled his big friendly smile, I didn't want to disappoint him. It killed me to know that I absolutely would.

"You getting excited for tonight?" he added.

I nodded for what felt like thirty minutes as I built up the wherewithal to blatantly lie to this very kind man.

Finally, I let out a cheery "Yep!"

"Well, let's see what you've got!"

The room fell silent in my ears as the crinkling of the plastic bag got way louder than seemed possible from me digging out the ugly prom dress. The horror immediately registered on Daryl's face, but he was too sweet to mention it, and instead said, simply, "Uh-huh. And what else?" I pulled out whatever was next, a surprise even to me, and revealed a long pair of black bell bottoms and a blue sequined poncho. Daryl tried his hardest to seem delighted, but by the time I got to the following outfit, a terrible sailor-style dress that would cut off around my knees, he couldn't hold back his disdain.

"Wow. Okay." He cleared his throat, presumably because he had nothing else to say, and asked to see my wig. I could feel everyone's eyes judging me as I pulled the pink wig out of my bag. Daryl's face turned as white as a sheet. He just kept nodding and repeating the words, "Okay, great. Good." Then moved on to the next guy.

I was very, very, very screwed.

Seth had stayed waiting in the alley for me, so when I finished with Daryl and had a fifteen-minute break, I went out to tell him how it had gone. I didn't have the heart to tell him that the horror people had shown on their faces was equal to what you'd see from people watching one of those Paranormal Activity movies or *Sex and the City 2* for the first time. I lied and said it had gone okay and that I was feeling not quite as freaked out.

Really, though, I had just resolved myself to defeat, and was quietly coming to terms with it.

One more run-through of the opening number, and then we were on our own until showtime. I was too nervous to eat food before the show. I was in a pretty calm, resolved place about the fact that I would be the worst-dressed person in the pageant, and on top of that, maybe even the worst overall. Strangely, however, I felt like I had nothing left to lose. If I humiliated myself, Seth and Heather (if she showed up) were the only people in my life who'd know. The rest of the people—I'd never see them again. I'd lost my admission ticket to this brave new world. I would go back to my parents. Back to their blank stares and TV dinners. Back to the nothingness of my life in Florida.

Tash and I passed each other in the hallway. I tried to ignore him, but he stopped me.

"Excited?" he said in the phoniest voice I'd heard since Ariana Grande's last album. I kept walking, but he kept calling to me. "Hey. JT! Are you *excited*?"

I stopped, turned, plastered on a smile, and as bitchily as possible called back, "Oh, don't you know it!"

Then I kept walking, as I was fairly certain the alternative would've been to strangle him.

# chapter TWENTY-ONE

I DIDN'T SMOKE. I'D TRIED a cigarette once, when I was fourteen. I'd stolen it from my mom's purse, and smoking it had made me sick.

Still, that was what I found myself doing in the alley behind the building two hours before showtime. Smoking my second cigarette ever. It was nerves; it was peer pressure; it was the need for a fabulous gesturing prop.

Five of the other contestants and a few of the crew people were out there while I pretended not to want to vomit as I puffed the cigarette between my fingers. It was a necessary distraction from the panic I was feeling. I was an hour away from walking onstage looking like a homeless, bewildered showgirl in a sea of perfectly styled glamazons who knew exactly what the hell they were doing.

There was a bad traffic jam, not unlike the one I had caused on my first night in the city. People were honking and yelling, but we all ignored it as we discussed drag, our futures, and the awesomeness of New York City. That's why it took me so long to notice the person shouting my name, but finally, I did.

"JT! JT BARNETT! You put that cigarette out or I'm coming over there and wringing your neck!"

Finally I bolted up. It was the ghost of Nana calling down at me, and she'd chosen a real bad time to do so. However, as I looked around and into the sky, I noticed the black Escalade stuck in the traffic jam and the burst of orange hair shouting at me from the backseat window.

It was none other than Tina Travis.

It was like a cartoon. I rubbed my eyes to make sure I wasn't dreaming. Then I ran through the stopped traffic up to her window.

"Get in," she said. "This shit ain't going anywhere any time soon." She shouted among the shouting and honking. I got in.

"What're you doing in New York?!" I gasped.

She shrugged and told me she was a superstar and that New York was where she belonged. I couldn't argue that. She grabbed my knee and pinched it hard enough to bruise.

"Well, now I guess I have to kill you," she said, in the matter-of-fact way you'd say you need to water your plants or go pee, or kill two birds with one stone.

"Huh?"

"That thing you were smoking. I told you . . . with that voice of yours!"

I tried explaining it was only because I was super stressed and nervous, but she wouldn't hear it.

"All you kids think you can just do whatever you want and that your voice won't go away. Sure, we did too in my day, only difference is that we didn't know any better. My generation was misinformed; yours is just plain stupid. You gotta choose one or the other, and, honey, I get it. Smoking might just beat out the singing BS."

That's when I decided to tell her everything.

"My costumes got stolen, Tina. And my wigs. Your stuff. This horrible person who I happen to be sharing an apartment with and who absolutely hates me, he stole them and he won't give them back, and if I tell the pageant he'll make it worse and I'm screwed. So I'm stressed, okay? I was having a cigarette and I know that's wrong and gross and nasty. I don't even like the taste, but everybody else seems to think they calm them down, so I was just hoping they might do the same for me. But even after I finished it, I was still just as screwed as I was before I started smoking it."

Tina squinted her beautiful green eyes at me, either in thought or for dramatic effect. Judging from the short time I'd known her, I ventured to guess it was the latter.

"Somebody stole your stuff?"

"Uh-huh."

"And you don't think you'll get it back?"

"Nope."

I explained that Seth had, very sweetly, spent the last of our money on some outfits and a cheap wig. As she tapped her long red fingernail on her chin, I could see the wheels in her head turning.

"Are you actually in New York just for the hell of it?" I asked.

"Watch your mouth!" She locked eyes with me for a while,

then finally let go with a shrug. "I'm here to see the pageant, dumbass."

"How did you even figure out where it was?"

"You think I wouldn't want to come see the first drag teen I'd ever met compete in *my* clothes and *my* wigs? I used to be famous. I've still got real powerful agents who can track down anything if I tell them to. Also, you left a pamphlet about the pageant in my garage apartment."

"But . . ."

"I know. You screwed up and lost my clothes and wigs, and unfortunately you need to pay to replace them."

I felt like I'd had the wind knocked out of me.

"I'm kidding! Lighten up, kid. Here. You need a dose of irony if you're going to be a drag queen. Calm down. You aren't even taking a second to appreciate the fact that I came all this way!"

"Oh. I'm sorry—you know how honored I am. I'm just distracted and worried about everything. It isn't you."

"Lord, you're freaking out again, aren't you?"

I nodded as she rolled her eyes, framed by fake eyelashes more ridiculous than those of any drag queen in the pageant.

"So, let's look at the facts. The big problem here is you don't have a good wig, huh?"

I shook my head, disappointed to have lost the incredible wigs she'd given me.

"And you don't have costumes?"

"Nope."

She reached into the backseat and grabbed a small suitcase, placing it in my lap.

"Here, wear these. That's the emergency suitcase I bring in case I decide to go perform somewhere, spur of the moment."

"Tina, I can't take more of your stuff."

"And take this." She pulled the red bouffant off and handed it to me, her almost-bald head revealed underneath. "Wear it . . . but if you so much as *think* of taking a photo of me without it right now, I'll make you wish you had never been born."

She tied the silk scarf around her neck into a turban, like the one Nana had worn during chemo. I ran my fingers through the gorgeous wig in my hands while something inside became completely calm, telling me that everything was going to be okay.

I had gotten my chance back. And another killer wig to boot.

Now I had to take it. The chance, not the wig.

Well, actually, both.

# chapter TWENTY-TWO

"MR. HART?" I CHASED DARYL down the backstage hallway. He was in a tizzy with last-minute preparations.

"Yes, JT?"

"I wanted to see if it's too late to change my costumes."

Daryl frowned and started to say something, then stopped himself. Looking around to make sure no one was listening, he whispered, "I'm supposed to say no, according to the rules, but follow me."

I followed him into one of the small dressing rooms off the stage, pulling Tina's suitcase behind me. He shut the door.

"You can't tell the others that I made an exception. Technically once your costumes have been approved, you're not supposed to change them. But after seeing what you had, I think I can make an exception. Ultimately, I'm in charge and can alter the rules if need be."

I unzipped the suitcase of Tina's outfits. Daryl was visibly taken aback. So was I.

"Wow. JT. These are really nice pieces of clothing. Where did you get them?"

"A friend." He pulled out a long aqua-colored beaded gown that looked to have been hand-stitched. It was extremely impressive, so impressive that I couldn't imagine why Tina would have packed such a thing, even to maybe perform in. But if there was one thing I had learned about Tina Travis, it was that she didn't need a reason to wear a floor-length evening gown. To be honest, that's something I had learned about almost everyone I had met in the past week.

"Well, all I can say is wow. Of course you should wear them."

"Thanks."

I packed the bag back up. Daryl started to leave, then stopped.

"Did something happen?" he asked. "Why did you have such terrible costumes earlier?"

"What do you mean?"

"Those costumes I saw earlier. They were, well, I think we can both agree they were worlds different from these, right? Seemed like something you threw together in a hurry. I mean, they had thrift store price tags on them. Someone didn't steal your original costumes, forcing you to have to piece together whatever you could find at the last minute, did they?"

With a tight smile, I shook my head. Daryl didn't break eye contact with me as he let himself out, adding, as we went out the door:

"Don't be afraid of Tash, okay? We all know that she's a basic bitch. And while basic bitches sometimes win a contest or two, they rarely win at life."

\* \* \*

I carefully guarded the new costumes for dear life in my little section of the dressing room. I had texted Heather and Seth with the big news; it was hard to fit the entire story into one text message, but I told them I'd fill in all the missing details later. Heather had texted me back with a series of rainbows, smiles, and ear emojis. While I was not entirely clear as to what that meant, I figured we were okay.

I was doing my makeup at the mirror, attempting to re-create the steps Bambi had shown me. I kept screwing up and starting over, but with each restart, I was getting a little bit better. I had just gotten my eyebrows covered up and my base on when the stage manager popped in to notify us that we were an hour from beginning. Milton and Red walked over, their drag half-done. They looked like the strangest team in the Olympics, each wearing panty hose, gym shorts, tank tops, and wig caps.

"*Bonjour!*" Milton sang to the tune of that song from *Beauty and the Beast*. "Are you stoked or are you stoked?!"

Milton was bouncing off the walls with energy, likely owing to the fact that he was sipping the largest can of Red Bull that I'd ever seen through one of those twisty straws. I explained that I was, in fact, very stoked.

"Hold the phone!" Red gasped as he saw my new costumes hanging from the rack. "Who the heck is *your* fairy dragmother?"

Red very carefully ran his fingers across the beads, like someone touching a great thousand-year-old Egyptian artifact. I blushed, wanting to tell them all about Tina but too afraid of word getting out.

"A friend of mine loaned them to me."

Milton and Red fawned all over the gowns, Red going so far as to Instagram a photo of them with the hashtag #*fashionheaven*, before going back to the mirror and finishing their makeup. Pip appeared, already in his first outfit, a flowing floral printed skirt with a fitted halter top made out of burlap or hemp or something else you could smoke. His straight blond wig went all the way down to his seemingly nonexistent butt.

"Salutations, dude. I have a gift for you." He placed a small crystal in my hand. "It's for good luck. It's a crystal found in an ancient Tibetan cave where a group of monks have lived for forty years in a vow of silence. Or at least that's what the girl at Urban Outfitters said."

I told him I didn't have anything for him, but he stopped me, launching into a long speech about how he didn't give me something to receive something, but to put forth the positive energy he hopes to live in himself . . . or something else that Deepak Chopra, Angelina Jolie, and Elmo would have approved of.

"The whole reason we're here, dude. Like, the whole thing . . . life or whatever . . . it's to try and make it a little bit better for the next person."

In the few days I'd known him, I had never heard him say a negative thing about anything or anyone. I couldn't remember the last time I'd gone an entire day without bitching at least a dozen times. I knew that I would probably never manage to be as positive as Pip, but experiencing his kindness, and reflecting on all that others had done for me in the past few days, made me want to try a little harder.

He gave me a big hug, wished me luck, and walked back to his makeup station, but not before shouting back to me, "Party!"

I made a mental note to include this kindness I had experienced in my speech . . . which was when it dawned on me that I *still* hadn't written it! I was just beginning to spiral into yet another wave of panic when there was a ridiculously loud crowing noise, followed by the unforgettably gruff guffaw of Lady Rooster.

She was standing in the doorway of the dressing room, decked out in the most stunning orange velvet gown, with the kind of enormous collar you'd see on a Count Dracula cape. Her wig was made entirely out of actual rooster feathers. She looked like Big Bird's aunt from South Florida.

"Helloooooo, my ferocious drag teens! Mother has arrived!" Many of the other contestants clapped and cheered, excited to see Lady Rooster in person. "Who in here is ready to give these rich old gay people the best drag show they've ever seen?!"

We all cheered some more, the energy building and building with each moment. As I looked across the room at all these guys from so many different places, I thought about just how cool all of this was. We had all found one another, found our brothers in drag, our sisters in fierceness, even those we didn't get along with—there was still a connection to celebrate. My eyes landed on Tash, in the corner of the room, looking uncharacteristically petrified. I saw, in his hand, the cause of his panic: a broken heel. My immediate reaction was a feeling of karma finally working correctly . . . but as I watched him spiral, I couldn't help but feel bad for the guy, and see more than just a little bit of myself in him. Maybe Pip was rubbing off on me. I needed to be writing my speech, and beyond that, I had every right to hate Tash, but I couldn't just stand there and watch as everyone ignored his hysteria. So I walked over.

"Tash?"

He looked up from his seat, where he was furiously attempting to glue the heel back to the bottom of his shoe, with no luck.

"What do you want?" he spat.

He was clearly in no mood to chat. So, the usual.

"Did you break your shoe?" I asked.

"What does it look like? Stupid, cheap things can't handle even one day of rehearsal."

I stood there quietly for a moment as he kept trying to fix it, getting progressively more frustrated by the second.

"I have extra shoes. Do you want to borrow them?"

He froze, staring down at the shoe for a minute or two, then looked up at me. "Why would you do that?"

I shrugged. "Because you need a shoe."

"But why would you do that? Nobody here even likes me."

He had a solid point there.

"Why do you think that is?" I asked.

"Because I'm a bitch."

Again, a solid point.

"And why is that?"

"Why is what?" he asked, throwing the broken shoe down to the ground and standing up to face me, eye to eye.

"Why are you a bitch?"

He looked shocked by the question.

I pressed on. "I've been nothing but nice to you since I met you, and you've been nothing but a bully. At first I thought, okay, maybe it's just me, but it's not. You're a bitch to everybody for no reason, and it's like, why? What's your problem?"

He nervously chewed his bottom lip, smudging his pink lipstick. After a while, he finally spoke, softer than ever before.

"The first time I ever dressed up in drag, I felt amazing. Right? I felt like a superstar—and I *was*. I dominated the night. I went to this party, right? And everybody wanted a photo with me because I looked really damn fine, and somebody posted a photo on Facebook. I didn't mind, because it racked up so many likes. Then when I came home, my dad comes into my bedroom, and he has the picture opened up on his phone. He shoves it in my face and starts yelling, saying what the hell is wrong with you, calling me a freak, telling me I'm disgusting. And right there, before I could even defend myself, he asked if I was gay, and I said yeah, and he got so mad I thought he was going to kill me. But he just took his fist and punched me, really really hard, across my face. Then he left my room, and I could hear my mom crying, telling him to apologize, and I could hear him calling me these awful words. I got a Lean Cuisine out of the freezer and held it on my face and I cried. And then, when it got really late, my mom came into my room and told me I had to leave. She couldn't stop crying, but she was just as scared of Dad as I was. So I left. I never saw them again. All because of some stupid wig I wanted to wear." He shook his head with a bemused and heartbroken laugh. "Holy hell. Does it get any more clichéd than that?"

He focused his damp eyelids down at the broken shoe and, after a moment, kicked it angrily across the room.

"That night I made up my mind. I decided screw it . . . I'll *be* a superstar, and nobody will stand in my way, ever. I'll never let somebody pretend to care about me ever again because at the end of the day, they're just another something between me and superstardom. And I've never forgotten it."

It was quiet for a while, except for the sounds of hair dryers and iPod speakers playing pop music around the room.

"Half hour till curtain," the stage manager announced on the sound system.

I handed Tash a pair of shoes. He didn't look up as he took them; he just stayed staring down at the ground.

"Not everybody is pretending, Tash. Some of us actually mean it."

He looked up at me, just a little bit, not all the way, and I could see that his mascara was creating long black squiggly lines as it ran down his cheeks, like the doodles in an algebra notebook. He mouthed the words "Thank you"—moved enough to acknowledge me, but not secure enough to let anyone else hear it.

"Hey, papi!" a contestant named Angel's Beth called out amid a cacophony of *ooohs* and whistles. I looked up to discover that the object of these catcalls was none other than Seth. He looked beautiful, as usual, but especially so now, in a plaid skinny tie and gray suit jacket that was just the slightest bit too small for him. His hair was slicked back like some handsome movie star from the old movies I'd watched with Nana. As soon as he saw me, his face lit up.

"Wow," he said. "JT, you look amazing."

He handed me a big bouquet of flowers wrapped in plastic. He'd forgotten to peel off the price tag, so I saw they'd cost him twenty-six bucks.

"Seth, you didn't have to do that."

He pulled me toward him, his breath minty as always.

"Shhhhh," he said. "This is the story of a boy about to win his own future. And in that story, the boy who loves him brings him flowers." He paused, looking a little nervous. "Am I allowed to kiss you, or is that going to screw up your makeup?"

I leaned forward and gently placed my lips on his in response. I could feel his lips turn up into a smile beneath my own.

"How do you feel?" he quietly asked, without moving his lips away from mine.

"Excited—well, excited and scared."

He pulled away from me, looking me up and down, taking in my whole outfit. I was in the red bouffant, some costume jewelry, and the aqua beaded gown—which was a little small, but if I didn't breathe too heavily, it was almost comfortable.

"You look beautiful. Really. All you need to do is go out there and show them the guy I fell in love with. Deal?"

"I haven't written my speech. Every time I've started to, something has happened. I don't know what I'm going to do."

Seth rolled his eyes. "Have you learned anything in the past few days?"

"Absolutely."

"Okay, then. All you need to do is go up there and tell everyone what you've learned. That's it."

"But it's a speech! Everyone has theirs memorized and funny."

"I'm not going to put my hand over your mouth because, again, I don't want to screw up your makeup. But listen to me. You go out there and tell us why you drag, from your heart. I know that heart, JT. And if you'll just allow everyone to see it, you're going to shine. Okay?"

I half nodded, half adjusted my wig.

"No. Say *okay*."

I whispered "Okay" as the stage manager called five minutes until showtime.

"Also, I got you this." He handed me an envelope. "Open it."

Inside was a piece of paper on which, in Seth's perfect handwriting, was a list of at least fifty random words and sentences.

"It's every possible secret I've never told you. Every skeleton in my closet."

*I don't actually like to work out. I always have to double check how to spell* February. *I don't know the difference between Jessica Alba and Jessica Biel,* I read from the list. Seth blushed.

"Yeah. Some secrets are juicier than others."

We laughed the kind of laugh people share when they're moved by the same thing, by each other. I felt silly for having been upset with Seth's secrets to begin with. We all have crap we bury; some of us have better shovels than others.

"I'm sorry," I said. "I never should have freaked out about all that. I've been really selfish."

Seth smiled. "You have been. Maybe we both have. But I'm glad. It's about damn time you did something selfish for once. I'm proud of you."

He pulled me into his arms one more time, then took one step back, snapping a photo.

"I better get out there. Heather's meeting me in the lobby. Apparently she's spent the day sleeping off last night. But I'll see you on the other side. Just shine, JT. Shine like you do for me every single day."

He walked away, through the other contestants. One queen whispered loud enough for the entire room to hear, "Screw the scholarship—they ought to give *him* as the prize!"

My heart fluttered.

"Final call to places, final call!"

# chapter TWENTY-THREE

THERE WAS A LOUD MURMUR from the audience as they took their seats on the other side of the big red curtain. All of us, all twenty contestants, were lined up in our staged formation for the opening number. I hadn't felt like this since waiting to go on for the school talent show. The difference was that here I was waiting to go on with nineteen other guys eager to embark on the same thing as me, and not a single one of them was a stupid football jock making lame jokes about me being gay.

I scanned the group. I saw Pip chanting something to himself. I saw Milton doing elaborate stretches like he was Natalie Portman in *Black Swan*. I saw Red walking through the choreography and singing the lyrics to himself. And I saw Tash, in the extra set of shoes, standing still, ready to unleash his inner diva.

Everyone looked great, truly not a single dud in the mix— except maybe Katy Hairy, who looked like a pirate lounge singer and was about as balanced as a pirate in a sea-tossed ship.

The work lights went out, the stage now almost entirely black, with the only light coming through a tiny crack in the curtain and a couple blue lights spilling over from the wings. Daryl weaved through us up to the front of the stage, right where the two curtains parted. Before going out, he turned around to face us.

"Folks, I just want to say, before we begin, that I couldn't be more excited for tonight." He spoke in a loud whisper. "I think this is one of the best groups of contestants we've ever had, and that's not something I say every year. Okay, yes it is. But this year I actually mean it."

The more nervous of us laughed.

"I want you to remember to go out there and have fun and be your true selves, okay? Show me everything that's inside of you. As you all know, John Denton wasn't just a brilliant playwright and performer, he was the first person who taught me that sometimes it takes stepping into someone else's shoes—namely, stilettos—to feel comfortable enough to let your true inner goddess shine through. Let's honor John tonight. Let's fill this room with our goddess energy and celebrate everything that's just plain fabulous about ourselves. How about it?"

This time, everyone but Tash cheered. Tash was a statue of poise.

"All right—let's do this!"

Daryl slipped through the part in the curtain, a spotlight hitting him as he did so, the hot white light seeping through. He launched into a speech welcoming the audience, talking about what the John Denton Foundation did and how the evening would work. He explained that after the opening number, the judges would whittle us down to ten contestants. The audience sounded lively and ready for a great show; it was intoxicating to hear their laughter and applause.

I couldn't wait for that curtain to part and those lights to hit me. I was ready. I was ready to introduce the world to . . . crap. It suddenly dawned on me that I still hadn't come up with a drag name. It hadn't come to me the way Bambi told me it would. There had been no sign, no act of drag God, no aha moment. Just a lot of things falling apart and me freaking out about every single one of them. I had been so busy discovering myself that I hadn't had a chance to discover my drag name.

But maybe that was the exact point.

RuPaul, one of the greatest drag queens of all time, simply used her given name in her journey to superstardom. If I had learned one thing in the past few days, it was that drag didn't have to be pretending to be somebody else. It was about letting your inner diva out, saying "F.U." to your inhibitions, and allowing yourself to stand up and shine. If anyone had emerged, it was me. And that was exactly who I decided my drag teen would be.

Lady Rooster stood in the wings, awaiting her entrance as the Mistress of Ceremonies. She was quietly berating the sound guy for giving her a microphone with a cord as opposed to one that was cordless. She was furious, doing that whispering version of screaming where you're not whispering at all but not extracting as much voice as you would if you were actually screaming.

"Do you know who I am?! Would you hand Bette Midler a wired microphone and say, 'Sorry, it's the best we could do'? No! You wouldn't, because she'd throw a cup of hot coffee at you. In fact, go get Lady Rooster a cup of hot coffee to throw at you!"

Just then, Daryl's voice could be heard asking the audience to give a warm welcome to the host, Lady Rooster. Like a switch had been thrown, she dropped any trace of rage and pushed the sound guy out of her way, making her grand entrance to way more cheering than she probably deserved. The chastised sound man, looking very relieved, shrugged and walked away.

Lady Rooster spent a solid ten minutes getting the audience to applaud every single detail of her costume, down to her earrings and toenail polish (which wasn't even visible in her close-toed shoes). She was a handful, to say the least, and seemingly not the nicest person around, but her ability to win over an audience was undeniable. The lineup backstage stated she'd do a five-minute opening monologue, but by minute fifteen I could tell it was going to be a long night. She spoke of the infamous four key traits they'd be looking for: glamour, talent, heart, and soul. Then she said her own four key traits were cash, credit, accessories, and something that rhymed with *truckability*. Finally, she asked the audience to join her in welcoming the contestants of the Sixth Annual Miss Drag Teen Pageant. The curtains parted, the bright pink stage lights blinding my eyes for a second until my vision came back and I could see Linda at the piano, counting us down.

*Three, two, one* and we were off.

The lyrics of the opening number were all about introducing us as queens. Lots of lyrics about being glamorous, at one point rhyming *glamour* with *hammer* and *mascara* with *bad roots will scare ya*, in a lyric I could barely understand. Oh, and to get a better sense of the whole thing, just imagine an entire stage of teenage boys in drag singing the lyrics to the song's chorus, which were: *We're being born / you have been warned / tonight's the night / we drag it home!* (Thirty dollars to anyone who can explain what that even means.)

I was pleasantly surprised at just how well I was doing on the choreography, attempting to remember to smile while doing so, as the choreographer had continuously reminded us by shouting out supportive things like "Who paid to see the damn show? WE DID!" throughout rehearsal.

We formed our vertical line down the center of the stage, each taking our turn to step into the spotlight and up to the microphone to give our introduction. Katy Hairy was first, then Miss Hedini, then Milton, aka Electro Shock.

"I'm Electro Shock and I'm from Buffalo, New York. I can sometimes surprise you, but it's good for all of us to be a little shocked sometimes."

The audience clapped as more and more queens had their moment: Rachael Gay, Natasha, Mimi Pick Me, Baby Diva, Texas Alexus, Roxanne Roll. When Pip got up, he held up both fingers in peace signs and announced, passionately, "I'm Eartha Peace and I'm from Woodstock, New York. I believe in the power of love!"

I was three away from the front and getting more nervous with each passing contestant. By the time Lady Footlocker was explaining that she believed that children were our future, I was beginning to sweat. The closer to the spotlight, the hotter it felt. After Red—aka Red Sia—made his introduction, I took my place in front of the microphone.

"I'm JT and I'm from Clearwater, Florida. I may not be the best drag teen, but I love doing it. I want to love myself, and you know what? When I'm in drag, I think I actually might. I'm *so* excited to be here!"

I could hear Heather cheering from the back like some crazed football fan as I scurried back to my place.

As we finished the introductions and moved in opposite directions across the stage, I could feel one of the false eyelashes peeling off my eyelid. I attempted to keep it on by blinking uncontrollably, but I could feel it slowly peel farther and farther. Pretty soon I knew it was too late. It was a strange feeling too, like a cockroach you didn't know was hanging out in your eyelid was beginning to crawl out. Only it wasn't a bug at all but your entire eyelash. As the other contestants stomped their heels past me, I had my eyes focused on the ground to see where it had landed. I spotted it a little left of center stage—luckily no one had stepped on it, but it was, without a doubt, only a matter of time before someone did just that.

Within the staging, I wouldn't be passing that specific spot again for another verse. By then it could very well be too late.

I got to stage right, where my group of ten had to strike a pose, complete with silhouette and jazz hands, and belt the Dr. Seuss–like lyric *Wigs on our heads and brains underneath / we're more than just beauty queens, more than lipstick and teeth.* On the downbeat, we all flashed our best pageant smiles and fluttered our eyes at the laughing audience, but mine were shifting back to the sole eyelash, lying there motionless like some tragic fallen soldier.

I looked around, hoping to catch another queen's eyes, to signal *MAYDAY!* But no one noticed me. We crossed the stage once more, past the eyelash . . . but I was in the back row and couldn't reach it. It was out of sight for a while at a part where I really, really needed to concentrate on my kick step. When I got to the left side of the stage, I looked back . . . and it was gone!

The music was building, as a strange soundtrack to my own building blood pressure. I scanned other areas of the stage, but with no luck. It was nowhere to be found. It was likely on the bottom of someone's plus-size stilettos, and I hadn't brought a spare. I wasn't going to let it deter me, however. *As soon as I get offstage*, I thought, *I'll rip off the remaining eyelash and that'll be my thing: the drag queen without eyelashes.* A lump of disappointment formed in my throat as all the contestants stepped into the two choreographed lines across the stage. As I passed Tash, I felt a tap on my shoulder. I looked behind me, and his eyes signaled down to his palm. There was my lost eyelash. I let out a gasp of relief and grabbed it. Tash winked and took his place in the front row, all of us hitting our marks and striking our designated poses for the final chord of the song, followed immediately by the stage lights blacking out and the audience erupting into applause.

Before the curtain could even close, Lady Rooster was already back onstage, in a new costume to introduce the judges. As she called each of their names, they walked from the back of the theater and took seats at a table in the corner of the stage. Quentin Brock was the first to be introduced; he looked older than I imagined he would be, even though he had been a celebrated playwright and screenwriter since long before I was born. He was mostly a cult icon, having had only one major hit as far as movies were concerned, an unintentionally campy movie called *Bad Girls with Good Hair* that starred a young Kim Cattrall as a supermodel who opens up a beauty salon in a small town outside Minneapolis after being dumped by her boyfriend. Her aim? To give the women of the town a new look *and* a new outlook. Various gays in the audience shouted what was arguably the most famous quote from the movie as Quentin took his seat: "I'm not a wizard—they're just good bangs!"

Next came Nathan Leary, who was dressed so formally it was almost annoying. The audience went really wild for him; it was impossible not to. One glimpse of Nathan Leary in front of an audience and you couldn't imagine him doing anything else. Also, he carried his Tony Award with him, just in case people needed a reminder.

"Wow!" he cried. "I haven't heard anyone *that* excited since I stopped wearing Speedos!"

"Speedo your butt into that seat, you ham with a side of eggs," Lady Rooster crowed. "Because last—but certainly not least—I'd like to introduce all of you to the newest board member here at the John Denton Foundation. He also happens to be one of the biggest movie stars in the world, and if he ever came into Lady Rooster's coop, it ain't eggs she'd be laying. Please give a barely legal welcome to . . . Samuel Deckman!"

Samuel Deckman made his way across the stage, all of us contestants piling into the wings to get a peek of the gorgeous superstar in person. Photos and movie clips didn't lie: Samuel Deckman was indeed the poster boy of handsome. He was taller than he looked on screen, with extremely broad shoulders, a perfect head of black hair, and the kind of clothes that would look expensive even next to someone with hundred-dollar bills taped all over him.

The audience oohed and ahhed as he walked across the stage, waving, blushing, and grinning at the affection. He took his seat next to Nathan Leary, who did a funny bit that got progressively longer and more elaborate as the audience laughed. By the end of the bit, Nathan Leary had managed to slide himself onto the floor and "pass out." Samuel Deckman got a big kick out of the whole thing; Lady Rooster, on the other hand, was far from enjoying the competition for laughs.

"If you want to get him to polish your Tony, do it on your own time," she interrupted. "It's time now to call ten of our contestants to the stage. Egg roll, please!"

The atmosphere backstage changed in an instant, as Lady Rooster began calling names to the stage. It was unclear whether these were the contestants going home or the ones staying, and Lady Rooster was loving every second of our fear.

"Sandra Buttock. Mimi Pick Me. Annie Body. Texas Alexus. Katy Hairy."

With each name, the corresponding trembling drag teen joined the line across the stage until Lady Rooster reached the tenth name, Dorothy Kale. The remaining ten of us backstage paced back and forth, waiting to find out if it was us or them going home.

Finally, Lady Rooster spoke. "As you all know, we must cut ten contestants at this point. So will these remain? Or will these, sadly, have to go home? This is one of the toughest parts of the night. Before we go further, I want to say again that all twenty of these drag teens are stars. So let's give them another round of applause."

After all the applause died down, Lady Rooster spoke slowly.

"This group of ten, I'm sorry to say, is going home."

Various *aw*s and boos came from all over the room as each of the ten contestants' hopes were dashed. I could feel for them, but I was also incredibly relieved. The rest of us retreated to breathe and to change into our next outfits. We were all very quiet as we reentered our dressing room, a rarity for this group. It was as if we'd all just survived a plane crash and were processing it, slowly but surely.

I was still late in the lineup, so I had some time before my talent portion. I changed into my outfit, a very flashy Western-style shirt that absolutely screamed Tina Travis, and not just because it belonged to her. I wore one of her big chunky belts at the waist across a short sequined skirt underneath, with the most dazzling high-heeled cowboy—or cow*girl*—boots ever created. *Dazzling* might seem like a bit much when describing boots, but they were bright blue leather with orange stitching and what appeared to be diamonds on the toes. (With anyone else I'd have guessed them to be rhinestones, but with Tina there was no way to be sure.) They were *way* too small for me, and for a brief period in the process of squeezing my fat feet into them, I thought they might never come off again without calling in the Jaws of Life.

I made my first attempt at walking in them as I took a test

stroll around the dressing room; each step felt like someone was squeezing my feet and breaking them with their bare hands.

"Ouch. Crap. Jesus. Ouch," I was muttering to myself as I wandered around in circles, almost bumping into Milton as he walked in after finishing his talent, which was juggling three lit torches. "Whoops. Sorry. How'd it go?!" I looked over and saw that Milton was holding his wig, which was smoldering with smoke and ash. "I'm going to guess not well?"

He tossed the ruined wig in the sink and turned on the faucet.

"Eh. Whatever. It's my own fault. Why didn't I think about hair spray being so flammable?"

This was a good question, but I didn't think he needed me to reiterate it, so I refrained.

"Well, did they at least like it?"

"Oh yeah!" He brightened up. "Nathan Leary said it was the most flamingly perfect thing he'd encountered since the premiere of *Mamma Mia!* I need to go dig out my hat to wear for the rest of the pageant. Good'luck, honey!"

From onstage, I could hear the tail end of Roxanne Roll's performance, which meant I was three performances away. Roxanne was playing what she called a song but what really sounded like a fatal car accident on an electric guitar. I hadn't spoken to her much throughout the pageant—but besides the DEATH TO POP tattoo on her right forearm, she'd seemed perfectly nice.

I hobbled into the alley to do a vocal warm-up, each step cutting off my circulation even more. The alley was quiet, except for the sounds of New York City traffic going by. I looked around to make sure no one was listening and then let out an enormous belt. My "Ahhhhhh" echoed off the fire escapes and Dumpsters.

I did another long, loud scale, rubbing my jaw to loosen it like singers do when they want people to notice that they are singers. Then I started to run through the song.

"*I was never the type of girl, the type who knew what she wanted / I was never the type of girl, the type who didn't listen when she was taunted / I always felt alone, and—*"

"SHUT UP! I'm trying to sleep!" a voice rang out from a window overlooking the alley. I stopped abruptly. And before I could shout back that I was sorry, another voice screamed from behind me, "No, YOU shut up! He's rehearsing!"

It was Tina, jogging down the alley toward me, zigzagging in her high heels on the uneven bricks.

"I thought you were watching the show?" I said.

"I am, silly. And you're doing great. But I was sitting there watching that one fella whose wig caught on fire and thought about how I'd kill you if that happened to the one you're wearing. Then I realized I forgot the most important part of your ensemble!"

She plopped a sequined cowgirl hat on top of my head.

"*Now* you look perfect."

I thanked her and hobbled back inside as she ran back down the alley, whooping the whole way.

＊　＊　＊

I took my place in the wings as Pip finished up his talent. He did an interpretive dance to "Colors of the Wind" in a purple unitard that he claimed was a commentary on global warming and "The Middle East." The audience gave him a friendly round of applause but I could tell it had gone a bit over their heads. The judges tried to give him their best and shortest criticisms.

"Innovative!" said Quentin Brock.

"Beautiful," said Samuel Deckman.

"Funny, I don't remember taking LSD," Nathan Leary deadpanned.

As Pip passed by me on his way off the stage, he squeezed my hand. "You're going to be wonderful, dude."

I smiled at him as I heard my name being said and the crowd beginning to applaud.

"All the way from Clearwater, Florida—where the hell is that?" Lady Rooster announced. "JT!"

The interlude of "People Care" began as I nervously walked out onto the stage, slowly—and not for dramatic effect, but because that was just as fast as I could move in the too-small boots. I got to the microphone, to my fate, to another potential humiliation. I looked down at Linda Lambert at the piano, and she winked at me as she began to play the verse and I began to sing.

*I was never the type of girl,*
*the type who knew what she wanted.*
*I was never the type of girl,*
*the type who didn't listen when she was taunted.*

*I always felt alone, and that was just all right with me,*
*until one day, I looked around*
*and realized how lovely life could be . . .*

The lights were still so bright it was hard to see, but I made a point to actually look around, and really take in my surroundings for the first time all night. What I was doing was extremely cool, and I was extremely lucky to be JT Barnett in that moment.

*Tried before and I failed.*
*Thought I knew, but that boat sailed.*
*Tried to find the real me*
*and I just couldn't see.*
*Now every day is a blessing,*
*every day a new try,*
*a chance to find yourself,*
*find the reason why.*

On the key change, I noticed the other contestants in the wings watching. It almost threw me off, but I stopped those tired old fears and used them, made them my fuel. I yanked the microphone out of the stand and walked down to the lip of the stage, like I'd seen famous singers do on TV.

I saw Heather and Seth seated in the middle of the theater. Heather waved at me, like a mom watching her kid in a dance recital. Seth beamed. It was clear that in his eyes, I really *was* shining. I almost started to laugh. As I walked across the front of the stage, I felt like more of a diva than I'd ever felt before. I was so in it that my feet weren't even hurting. Or maybe they had just completely lost all feeling—either way, I felt great!

> *People care about me,*
> *which I sometimes forget.*
> *People care about me,*
> *and that's as lucky as you get.*
> *Everybody!*

Suddenly, everyone was singing along, even people who didn't know the words. It was amazing, everyone was focused on me, and not a single one of them was doing it to make me feel bad about myself. By the final chorus, the room was vibrating with the sound of everyone's booming voices. I even spotted Lady Rooster mouthing along in the wings.

> *People care about me,*
> *which I sometimes forget.*
> *People care about me,*
> *and that's as lucky as you get!*

At the end, they leapt to their feet—like actually, they really did. They leapt to their freaking feet.
It felt utterly spectacular.

# chapter TWENTY-FOUR

ONCE I GOT OFFSTAGE, EVERYONE was coming up to me and telling me congratulations. I was attempting to take it all in, but my mind wasn't entirely clear just yet. I still had to do the speech I hadn't written.

I was soon busily changing into my next and final gown. I couldn't believe just how fashion-forward Tina's outdated wardrobe was coming across, the final gown being at least thirty years old. It had a really high collar, it was sleeveless (something I was NOT thrilled with), and it had this Southwestern-looking pattern, like a Navajo print, the kind of pattern you'd see on a throw pillow from Anthropologie. It was definitely the tightest of all three things I'd put on, and I thanked God I hadn't tried to sing in it.

"Could somebody help zip me?" I called out to the room. Red looked up from his mirror, where he was reapplying some eye makeup.

"Over here, JT!" he called.

I turned my back to Red and winced at a glimpse of my back fat pouring out. Red grabbed hold of the zipper.

"Try not to breathe!"

I took a final gasp and held my breath as he yanked once, then again, then again, then again.

"Is it stuck?"

"Um . . . you could say that."

I looked back in the mirror. It was stuck all right, but it wasn't the zipper's fault. It was the fault of all those Wendy's fries. Or fries from McDonald's. Or Arby's. Or, if there was no other option, Burger King.

"Crap. It's not going to work, is it?"

Red got an idea. "Hold on. I'm wearing something really loose for my speech. Unzip me."

I obliged, albeit very confusedly, as Red stepped out of his gown. He was wrapped in something that looked like an enormous and highly uncomfortable Ace bandage.

"What the hell is that?"

Red began shimmying the contraption over his head. "They're Spanx. Duh."

"Oh," I said, attempting to sound like I had any clue what he meant. He was in disbelief that I didn't.

"You don't know what Spanx are? Come on. Everybody knows what Spanx are! Don't you watch any daytime women's talk shows?"

I shook my head in understanding because I did. I'd just never seen the oft-discussed Spanx in person.

"They're the greatest invention ever made. Better than the lightbulb, better than the Internet, better than frozen yogurt. You slip this bad boy on and everything gets sucked up into one nice tight roll. Think of your body as a bunch of fatty beef and this as a sausage casing."

The image was less than appealing, but I took the Spanx anyway. Red helped me slide into it. Did you ever hear that story about the guy who passed out drunk in India and, while he was passed out, got swallowed by an enormous cobra? There was even a photo—it was all over Facebook and forever stopped me from going to India, and for a brief period, ever going on Facebook again. Anyway, that was what putting on these Spanx felt like.

"Now let's try the dress again." Red helped me step into the dress and pull it back up around me. Then, as if I were a size zero in a size ten, the zipper went up without any struggle whatsoever.

"Jesus Christ!" I shouted.

"I know!"

Red walked over to his rack of costumes, beaming with pride like a dad who'd just taught his son how to hit a baseball, and put on his gold blouse.

"You ready for your speech?" he asked me.

"We'll see." I spoke to him through the mirror as he finished changing. "I didn't have time to write one, but I'm just trying to trust that I'll get up there and know what to say. Speak from my heart and soul or whatever."

Red stepped beside me. We were both looking at each other in the mirror, each of us looking not just like drag teens but, honest to God, legit, glamorous drag queens.

"Sounds good to me. After all, JT, isn't your heart and soul the whole point?"

Public speaking is basically the worst possible thing to put any human through unless they're famous, in which case, people will listen to absolutely anything you say even if it makes literally no sense. This was evidenced by Samuel Beckman, who, while very, very handsome, was quickly proving himself not to be the sharpest tool in the shed. He'd asked one performer, after they finished lip-synching to Cher's "Believe," who had originated the song. He was met with a cacophony of boos and actual hisses.

The judges had been all around really kind throughout the evening, aside from a few snide jokes from Nathan Leary, but even then it was clear it was in good fun. Lady Rooster and Nathan Leary had officially had enough of each other, both exhausted from competing for the attention of the audience.

For this final part of the evening, they had chosen a new order. At the moment, Roxanne Roll was finishing up her speech, which basically consisted of her screaming "rock 'n' roll!" at the audience a lot, and bragging about how she wasn't part of the "gay system," whatever that was.

I'd gotten to hear a few snippets throughout the speeches. Milton had given a long speech about hoping to follow in RuPaul's footsteps as a fashion icon, and had even added a joke about how proud he was to be a flamer. Pip had spoken briefly, and poetically, about how drag is like being a flower.

Tash was waiting on the other side of the stage, ready to go on, as Roxanne Roll finished. The audience clapped politely, and I could see more than a few of them actually scratch their heads.

"Wow! Well, that was something, huh?" Lady Rooster joked as she came back to the stage. "I can't say that I mind she's not a part of *my* gay system. Up next, we've got somebody I've seen on the drag scene since she was a tiny little drag preteen—hey, that rhymed! I should be writing the Broadway musicals! Right, Linda?" Linda, still seated at the piano, smiled politely, obviously as exhausted by Lady Rooster as the rest of us were. "Anyway, please make some room for our next little bitch, Natasha!"

Tash walked out, grand and regal.

"Good evening. I am legendary, I am divinity, I *am* Natasha!" Tash spoke way too loudly, and a little too proudly, into the microphone. She didn't seem to care—but the audience, however, did. I could see a few of them shifting uncomfortably in their seats.

Tash went on to give what was clearly a memorized speech. It was all done in his usual persona, and when there were jokes, he got laughs, and when he called out for responses, he got responses. But overall it felt so formulaic, so routine, so the Tash I'd met in the apartment. It was worlds away from the Tash he'd revealed to me, the Tash who had cracked out of the perfectly formed drag teen he'd built around himself.

"Greetings, Earthlings. I come from the Planet of Natasha, in the galaxy of fabulous, in the universe of . . ." She didn't stay a word here but instead snapped her fingers and vogued her arms into a spasm that was at once revelatory and violent.

"I come to this pageant to pick up what is rightfully mine—the crown! Miss Drag Teen is in my blood. Along with fierceness, divinity, pizazz, and electricity. You want Miss Drag Teen to matter? Well, honey . . . now it does!"

Her speech dragged on with self-congratulatory comments like, "My soul is made up of the same stuff as Beyoncé and Miss Heidi Klum. You prick us and we bleed *beauty*."

I couldn't help but be disappointed. I thought I'd gotten through, broken past whatever guard he had, but the reality was that guards, when left standing long enough, get harder and harder to break. I made a promise to myself that no matter what, no matter the nerves, no matter the inhibitions or insecurities, I would break mine. I would break that heavily built guard and go out there and show me, show the real me, not just the me I wanted to show them, but all of it. Because that's what drag meant to me . . . the truth. Sugarcoated, for sure, but the truth above all else.

I heard my name being called to the stage. Everything seemed to be in slow motion as I walked back toward the microphone.

"Hi. Wow. Does this look as bright out there as it does up here? They've really got to figure that out. The stage lights blinding you, I mean. At the very least, I'm going to need an eye exam after this, so if you're an optometrist, leave your card."

My first laugh—a good one too.

"My name is JT. As I mentioned earlier, I hadn't really done a lot of this before tonight—only once before, actually. On my way here, I didn't have a drag name, and I still don't. JT is my actual name. Somebody told me to make my drag name what spoke to me, and I don't know if I'm lazy or not, but whatever the reason, the only name that spoke to me was my own."

My second laugh.

"And that's not coming from a diva place or whatever—it's just, I don't know . . . what I feel. Somebody told me that the great thing about drag is that it allows you to be the you you're afraid of letting loose, the you inside of you, and that's exactly what I feel like I've done. Up until tonight, I've never felt comfortable in my own skin. But tonight, as I walked onstage to do this, as I felt this crowd, as I sang, danced in the opening number, I felt . . . well, I don't know how to describe it, but right now I feel like I am exactly where I am supposed to be. More than any other time in my life."

I adjusted my wig.

"I love being a drag teen. I do. And I hope that one day I'll be a drag queen. But I just want to say that within the past week, I've learned so much. Not just about drag, but about myself, my fears, my insecurities, my passion, and what allows me to feel okay. And do you want to know what that is? It's putting on a wig and some mascara and heels and shining before an audience. I am such a terrified human being. I worry about what other people are thinking so often that I dream about it. The minute I step into a room, I assume you don't like me— or hate me, even. And sometimes that's the case. Sometimes people hate me. Sometimes they don't notice me. And I used to think that's all I wanted, to blend in. But if I've learned anything this week, it's that a lot of people not only notice, but they care. And that feels so much better than blending in ever has. Maybe I'm only half a drag queen, or half a boy, or half a something . . . but I want the world to meet JT. Sometimes JT looks like this. And sometimes he looks like this."

I pulled my wig off and fussed with my hair. Then I put the wig back on. Flawlessly.

"But sometimes, this wig, this eyeliner, this all-of-it . . . it's just the boost of confidence I need to feel really and truly and happily me. And so that's who I am, JT. We all need our own form of drag sometimes, to wrap ourselves up in, as we brave the frontier of self-discovery. There's been a lot of talk in this pageant about the four key words: glamour, talent, heart, and soul. I found the first two moderately quickly. Those you can rehearse. But the final two—well, that took coming here and doing this to solidify."

I cleared my throat.

"Heart. I have the sweetest and most beautiful boyfriend in the world, truly. I'd ask him to stand up if I weren't afraid of all of you stealing him."

The crowd laughed and looked around.like dogs for a treat that had just been tossed into the yard.

"And soul. I've realized that all of this . . . performing, letting go, feeling beautiful, feeling loved . . . that's my soul. That's everyone's soul. And I've found that here, a happy equation of it all, which I suppose is the whole point of tonight. Despite every setback, every failure, every mishap and freak-out . . . here I am. JT. Take me or leave me, wig and mascara and all. I'm just JT, and that's why I drag."

As I stepped away from the microphone and the audience applauded, I caught a glimpse of Daryl in the wings.

He was giving me a thumbs-up.

# chapter TWENTY-FIVE

THERE WAS A SHORT INTERMISSION as the judges deliberated. The ten of us gathered in the dressing room, making idle small talk, each of us too focused on what would happen in the upcoming ten minutes to have any form of real conversation.

Pip asked to lead us in a group meditation, but no one really jumped at the idea. A few of the contestants kept to themselves; Roxanne Roll and Miss Hedini chain-smoked on the fire escape, while Tash kept touching up his makeup in the mirror. From the way that he wasn't looking up and was avoiding conversation with everyone entirely, I could tell he wanted to be left alone.

Lady Rooster was pacing back and forth in the hallway, on her phone, angry with someone about something having to do with a gay cruise and somebody named Charo. The music began to play on the stage, and the stage manager called us to our places, each of us jittery and wishing each other halfhearted good-lucks.

We formed our line of ten across the stage as the judges all smiled at us, with the tension of knowing that nine of us would soon hate them. I kept telling myself that winning wasn't the point—the point was all that I had learned about myself in the past week.

But let's be honest: I wanted that scholarship.

Daryl returned to the stage thanking everyone, again, for their support, and announcing that the evening's tickets and donations had raised a grand total of one hundred and fifteen thousand dollars, an amount of money that seemed so unfathomable to me that it might as well have been a million. He reminded us contestants that each of us was a winner, and all that other crap they always tell people in pageants. We each nodded and smiled politely, but it was clear that in each of our minds, the thought was the same: *Shut up and give me that crown!*

As if the wait hadn't been long enough already, the judges each gave their own little pep talk about how we were all some of the best young drag performers they'd ever seen. I was on the verge of exploding and shouting *Just tell us!* when Samuel Deckman said I had looked beautiful all night . . . at which point I briefly forgot about the pageant entirely.

Daryl introduced the currently reigning Miss Drag Teen, Princess Latifah, to the stage. She was a beautiful, very tall African American girl with the best makeup I'd seen all night. Her face was more than a perfect drag makeup job; it was a work of art. She wore no wig, but instead a shaved head, earrings that must have weighed at least ten pounds each, and the most beautiful gown I'd ever seen. She looked like an elegant Kerry Washington, but bald. She also had this air about her, like she wasn't one of us but instead a legit star, and not in an egotistical way.

"Princess Latifah, welcome back."

She bowed modestly to the audience. "Thank you, Daryl. It's lovely to be back among so many familiar faces."

"What has been the best part of your year in the crown, Latif'?"

She even looked regal while thinking. "Getting to see so many sides of the gay community and just how big and varied it is. It's easy, I think, as a young queer person, to not feel like you belong to your queer brothers and sisters, because maybe you've never met the ones you identify with. If I've learned anything this year, it's that no matter who you are, where you are, or how you feel, there are people out there for you. This enormous community is its own tribe, but within that tribe are countless smaller tribes. If you open yourself up, you'll find yours."

It was as if Princess Latifah was speaking directly to me, but from the look on all my fellow contestants' faces, I could tell they were thinking the same thing. Which was a cool thing to realize, that we all feel like out-of-place weirdos even within what's supposed to be our own community.

"Well, Princess Latifah . . . are you ready to hand over the crown?"

Lady Rooster brought the results to Daryl, making a long, grand strut across the stage.

"Inside this envelope is the winner of this year's Miss Drag Teen Pageant," Daryl announced. "This contestant will win a full scholarship paid for by the John Denton Foundation, as well as hold the title and responsibilities of being Miss Drag Teen USA for the next year." All of us contestants joined hands. "And the runner-up will receive a cash prize of one hundred dollars and the responsibility of fulfilling all Miss Drag Teen USA duties if the winner should become unable to do so. Drum-roll, please."

The tension was so thick you could have cut it with a sharpened bobby pin.

"The runner-up of this year's Miss Drag Teen Pageant is . . . Red Sia!"

Red gasped and stepped forward as the audience applauded. Each of the rest of us looked more nervous and yet satisfied to have not heard our name called. Red thanked the audience over and over as he shook hands with Daryl and Princess Latifah.

"And now," Daryl proclaimed, "without further ado, the winner, the new Miss Drag Teen USA representing the John Denton Foundation is . . . Miss Hedini!"

The audience roared with applause and howling. Miss Hedini, immediately beginning to cry, stepped forward. The spotlight hit her and followed her to center stage, where she shook Daryl's hand and lowered her head before Princess Latifah, who ceremoniously placed her crown on Miss Hedini's enormous Afro. Daryl hung the sash over her shoulders, and Nathan Leary got up from the judge's table and gave her an enormous bouquet of roses. As she stood center stage, doing a perfect pageant wave, she looked beautiful. The other contestants and I, disappointed, made our way backstage.

It was over.

I'd given it my best shot, more than my best shot, and while I was really bummed, I couldn't help but feel extremely proud of myself. I thought back to when Seth had first introduced the idea of this whole adventure—I never could have imagined actually going through with it. But I did. I had.

A few of the contestants were angry, whispering snide insults about Miss Hedini to each other. Milton wasn't fazed; after all, I suppose few things can shock you after you've had a flaming wig on your head. I sat down in front of my makeup mirror to begin wiping my face off. But first I took one last look at my beautiful creation. I had a makeup wipe over my eyes when someone tapped me on the shoulder.

"Hey."

It was Tash. She was looking down, timid for the first time ever.

"Sorry you lost," she said.

"You too, Tash. You looked great."

She nodded, looking over her shoulder as if she was searching for what to say next. "Look. I just wanted to say thanks. No one's ever talked to me like you talked to me today."

"What do you mean?"

"Well, I guess no one ever really talks to me at all. And I just thought I should give these back." She handed over a trash bag; when I looked inside, I saw it was full of my missing costumes and wigs. "It was cruel and cowardly, I know. And if you never want to speak to me again, I get it. Why would you? But I just wanted you to know that I'm sorry and that I thought what you said out there, in your speech, was really cool. I don't think I would ever know how to be honest like that."

I didn't know what to say. What she'd done was indeed cruel and cowardly, but on some level I understood. Maybe I'd never sabotaged someone else because of my own fears and insecurities, but I'd certainly sabotaged myself, and who's to say what's worse?

Tash shook her head. "I couldn't do it. I couldn't speak from my heart or my soul. I guess I just don't know what they even sound like."

She was staring at the tiles on the floor, biting her lip, little smears of pink lipstick smudged across her front teeth, and I knew in my heart that I should forgive her. I pulled her toward me; she stood stiff and awkward in my arms. I could feel tears falling from her eyes onto my shoulders, and I kept her there as she whispered softly, "I don't remember the last time somebody hugged me."

"JT!!!!!" I could recognize Heather's scream no matter where I was. I pulled away from Tash to find Heather and Seth walking in. "You were amazing!!!"

Tash, wiping her eyes, nodded hello to them and scurried back to her station.

"Really, JT, she's right. You were incredible. So beautiful, babe." Seth hugged me so tight he cracked my back in that way he always does.

"How do you feel?" Heather was beaming, no trace of loser's remorse whatsoever.

"Ya know what? I feel okay. I feel pretty good, actually."

"She shouldn't have won. It is *so* ridiculous."

I cut her off. "No. It's not. Miss Hedini did a really great job, but you know what? So did I. And I didn't get a scholarship and that blows, but I did it. I actually did it. And right now, maybe I'm just a little high on the excitement, but I feel like that's enough."

Seth locked eyes with me, his sparkling like twinkly Christmas lights in the rain. Inside them I could see my own reflection. We stayed like that for a while as Heather launched into some argument about why Miss Hedini would be a completely forgettable flash in the drag teen pan. I just let her keep going because I could tell it was giving her joy.

"Hey, let's let you get changed and stuff. Meet us in the alley, okay?" Seth asked after a while.

"Okay. I'm *so* starving. I want to eat everything in New York City and some of the outer boroughs too."

Seth kissed me one more time.

"Hey, can I talk to you alone for a second?" Heather asked quietly.

Seth smiled and let himself out of the dressing room. Heather released a deep breath.

"Seth's already heard my apology, but I just wanted to say I'm sorry to you too, about freaking out and storming off like that last night." Heather was nervously shifting her weight from one foot to another. "I was being dramatic."

"Well, I certainly have no understanding what *that* is like," I joked.

She grinned. "Really, though. It was stupid of me to go off and meet that guy. I know you were just trying to protect me and that you don't think of me as just some fat-girl sidekick."

She handed me another makeup wipe.

"Thanks. I'm glad you realize that," I said, rubbing off my eye shadow. "Was it fun, at least? Your adventure?"

"It was. But I ditched Roger pretty quickly. You were right—he's a total creep."

"Then where were you all night?"

"Oh. With Daryl." Heather laughed, as if remembering something funny that you had to be there for. "Roger brought me to the club and was trying to get me drunk. He got *super* handsy, and when I asked him to slow dòwn, he got mad. So I kicked him in the crotch and told him to screw off. Daryl saw me and invited me to crash at his and Lady Rooster's place. We went out for cheeseburgers and ice cream at four a.m. and watched the sun come up over the river from their apartment window. It was legit perfection."

I gave her some serious side-eye.

"So do you still think gay guys hate women?" I asked.

"Not all of them." She grinned even wider. "I mean, some of you are total bitches, but the smart ones, you're better than anyone else."

She squeezed me so tight I felt my Spanx pop.

I finished taking off my makeup and changed back into my reg-ular clothes. I had spent only a few hours away from them, but it still felt strange to step into the shoes of just another regular person after so many hours of being a diva.

Red and Milton told me I had to come to the after-party, an annual event thrown at Daryl's loft for the contestants to celebrate and commiserate their losses. I told them that if there would be food, I'd consider it, but would need to talk to Seth and Heather first.

I packed up all the costumes, the wigs, the shoes, everything. It felt as if I were putting an entire little world I'd created for myself back into a bag, and I was sad to see that world go. As I headed out into the alley, I spotted Daryl by the door.

"Hey," I said.

He turned around with his big friendly smile and gave me another bear hug. "You were so wonderful, JT! You feel good?"

"Yeah. Really good. Hey, I just wanted to say thanks for taking care of Heather last night. We tried to keep her from going, but she was in rare form and, well, she's her own person."

Daryl squeezed my shoulder. "She's a great girl, JT. You're lucky to have her as a friend. Never take the girls in your life for granted. You hear me?"

"Deal."

Some powerful-looking couple pulled him into a conversation, but he shouted over to me as I walked away, "Come to the after-party! Bring your friends! And your family!"

"My family isn't here," I told him. But I said that if Seth and Heather weren't too tired, we'd stop by.

When I got to the alley, I found it was massively crowded, with everyone's supporters huddled around. It was funny how easily I could spot who was there for who, like the group of tough-looking people with piercings in places I didn't know you could pierce, who were clearly awaiting Roxanne Roll. I scanned the sea of people for Heather, Seth, and Tina . . . and when I spotted them, my jaw almost hit the pavement.

Because it wasn't just Heather, Seth, and Tina.

It was my parents too.

My mom and dad. Here.

Now.

"Surprise!" I couldn't hear her but I could read Tina's lips as I snaked my way over to them. They were smiling—visibly uncomfortable, but smiling nonetheless.

"Mom? Dad?"

"Hi, JT," Mom said. She and my dad couldn't have looked more out of place in this scene, or in New York City in general.

"What the . . . how did you know I was . . . I'm sorry, can someone explain what's going on?"

Tina cackled and shoved herself in between my parents, throwing her arms around them as if they were old friends.

"JT. After you left my house, I thought, damn, that's a kid who needs a mama and daddy to tell him he's going to be okay, not just some looney-tune old country singer. And after we'd had that talk about my folks and your folks, I just thought, what the hell? I'll track 'em down and fly them up to see the show."

I couldn't believe the words I was hearing.

I turned to my parents. "But weren't you surprised when you found out I wasn't in Daytona but in New York? Wait. Am I grounded?"

Dad shook his head. "We weren't all that surprised that you weren't actually in Daytona. To be honest, I reckon the idea that you would have wanted to go there in the first place was the weirdest part of all this. And you aren't grounded. You're going to be working your butt off at the gas station all summer, but you're not grounded."

I looked back at Heather and Seth for some semblance of reality, but they looked as bowled over with shock as I was.

"Besides, you're going to need that spending money at school, come fall," Mom added.

"But I can't. I mean, I didn't win and I . . ."

Tina stepped toward me with a look of mischief in her eyes. "Naw, you're going to school, JT. You might not have won over the dumb old judges of this pageant, but you won over dumb old me. You're going to college and I'm paying for it."

"WHAT?!" I shouted so loudly that everyone turned and looked at me.

Taking in the scene, someone's mom asked loudly, "Hey, is that Tina Travis?"

A couple of older gay guys pushed up toward Tina, losing their minds with excitement.

"Holy crap! You're Tina Travis!" a middle-aged man squealed like a child meeting Mickey Mouse. "Barry, get over here! It's Tina Travis! I'm sorry to bother you, ma'am, but my husband just loves you!"

Tina was basking in this star worship. She might have been one of the most grounded and levelheaded people I'd ever met, but she still had time to enjoy her fame. She stepped into the forming mob of excited fans, leaving me bewildered and overwhelmed.

"I can't believe this. I don't even know what to say. She . . ."

Seth stepped up beside me. "Sees how special you are, JT."

Mom looked nervous. I could tell she had something to say, but was afraid to speak up.

"You okay, Mom?" I asked.

She grabbed my hand, and for the first time since Nana's funeral, I saw tears in her eyes.

"We are so proud of you. You were so, so, so good up there, JT."

She pulled me in to hug her, and while I was in her arms, my dad wrapped his around the both of us. This was my definition of surreal.

"We love you so much. I'm sorry we have such a crappy way of showing it."

If somebody had told me a year before that I'd be standing in an alley in New York City, outside a drag pageant that I'd competed in, wearing Tina Travis's wig, hugging my parents and hearing them say they were proud of me . . . I never would have believed it.

But that's the funny thing about life, I guess.

You can't believe it till you live it.

# chapter TWENTY-SIX

DARYL'S LOFT WAS REALLY COOL, like nowhere I had ever been. It was a former factory or something that some gay guys with good taste made into a swanky apartment with super-high ceilings and amazing views of the Empire State Building.

All of the contestants were there, give or take a few who'd gotten really pissed about being cut after the opening number. There was a bar, but Daryl made it abundantly clear that no one under twenty-one would be allowed to drink in his home. I respected that, unlike almost of the contestants there (and Heather). There was room enough for a dance floor and DJ, where a few drag queens and the people who loved them were already dancing.

"Well, this is different," Mom said, looking around as we stepped off the elevator that opened directly into Daryl's loft.

"God almighty, you're telling me all of this place is his?" Dad was in disbelief. "I thought New York apartments were supposed to be tiny little holes in the wall."

"Not if you're rich." Tina stepped off the elevator. "That's the thing about New York City: It's a dump if you're poor, and absolute heaven if you're rich. Who's hungry? I see sliders!"

Tina led the way toward a table of food, which I was exceedingly thrilled to find. I filled my plate to the point of it being embarrassing and forced Seth to hold one of my egg rolls so I wouldn't look *too* ridiculous. Heather wandered off to gawk at the apartment.

"So. You think you'd like living in the Big Apple, JT?" Tina asked, with half a slider in her mouth.

"Oh yeah. I think that I'd love it."

Mom and Dad exchanged a somewhat sad look, and it weirdly made me feel good to imagine them missing me.

"What about you, Seth? You going to join him up here?"

Seth hesitated and began to speak, but I stopped him.

"He doesn't know that yet, Tina. Come on. Don't put him on the spot. We're seventeen . . . the most we can do is enjoy each other and the moment. Right?"

I could see Seth was a little surprised to hear those words come out of my mouth—but with a pleased expression, he placed his arm around my waist and agreed.

"Mrs. Travis?" Mom asked timidly.

"Tina, for God's sake!"

"Ha. Okay. Tina. Would you mind if we got a photo with you? Nobody at home is ever going to believe any of this."

Tina took out her phone, opened up the camera, and shoved it into the hand of a random person walking by.

"It'd piss me off if you didn't ask!" She got in between my parents, Seth and me squeezing in beside them. "And hey, you! Take it vertical so I can put it on my Instagram. That's what it's called, right?"

I laughed and said yeah. Then I said, "Wait! Heather, get over here!"

Heather looked up from the food table, where she was stopped in awe, like someone who'd just stumbled upon a pot of gold. "Coming!"

She got in next to us as Tina counted off the picture. *One, two, three.* She made the stranger keep taking alternatives. "Just in case you can see my turkey neck," she explained, grabbing her saggy neck.

After our spur-of-the-moment photo shoot ended, the music changed to something slow, and groups of people moved onto the dance floor.

"JT, let's dance." Seth tried pulling me behind him, but I protested.

"No, I'll look silly."

Seth put his hand on his hip and cocked his head to the side like he was posing for a nineties comedy album cover.

"You just spent two hours walking around in a seventy-something-year-old woman's wig and clothes in front of all these people, and *now* you're worried about looking silly?"

I couldn't argue with that.

"I heard that!" Tina shouted without looking up from her iPhone, where she was busily trying out different filters. "We won't post it with X Pro II. I look awful in that one."

"Come on!" Seth pulled me behind him, and when we hit the floor, we began to dance. Before long, my parents followed, dancing together in what was the first time I'd ever seen my parents dance. Or touch each other, for that matter.

"This is all so bizarre," I whispered.

"I know. Isn't it awesome?" Seth rested his forehead on mine.

From the corner of my eye, I saw Heather talking to a guy, one of the only guys there who didn't appear to be gay. She was laughing and flirty, and so was he. He seemed nervous the whole time they were talking, but then I saw Heather boldly grab his hand and pull him behind her. They began to dance, with her leading. We caught each other's glances and she shrugged, mouthing, "Oh well. Why not?"

Across the dance floor, I saw Milton and Red dancing together; Milton led, with Red towering over him as usual.

Tina didn't join us on the dance floor, or else it really would've been the perfect way to end this story. Instead she stayed back on the sidelines, surrounded by adoring gay guys, drag queens, and drag teens, signing autographs and taking selfies with all of them. She was in utter heaven.

I caught eyes with Tash, who had the nicest smile on his face. He was dancing with Pip, who appeared to be really "feeling the music." Tash blew me a kiss.

"You know what's going to suck?" I asked, my forehead still pressed against Seth's.

"Oh good. I'm glad you can still find something that sucks in this situation."

"Hey!" I playfully smacked Seth's butt. He chuckled. "I was just going to say that it's gonna suck having to go back to Florida, and real life, after all of this."

Seth looked around the room, surrounded by dancing couples of all genders, sexualities, appearances, races, tribes.

"Naw. It's not."

"It's not?"

"No. Because now we know what's out here. Now we know that no matter how low we ever feel, someday, this wonderful world of wonderfully weird and beautiful people, all of it, it's ours."

I looked around the room. He was right. Someday this would be my world. Sure, I'd be returning to Florida, to high school, to the gas station, but I'd been in the world I dreamed of being in. I'd found it, proving to myself that it actually did exist. And not only that, I also felt really and truly in the moment. Sometimes you have to wait a while to live in the exact world you dream of living in, and even then, it's never going to be exactly what you dreamed of once you get there. But the most you can do is be the person you dream of being, and once you find that person, the one who, no matter what happens, can dig deep inside himself and feel okay, you've found your world; you've found your otherwise.

And, finally, I'd found mine.

# acknowledgments

It's weird writing acknowledgments, because it feels like you're writing an Oscar acceptance speech, except you're not nominated for an Oscar. Or even a Daytime Emmy for that matter. Major thanks to David Levithan, whose books made me want to write books, and who I never imagined would end up being my editor. Equally big thanks to my reps: Scott Mendel, Kara Baker, and Cullen Conly. And to all the folks that make up my little circle of inspiration and support: Cole Escola, Jim Hansen, Drew Droege, Jordan Firstman, Bryan Safi, Orlando Soria, Edouard de Lachomette, Augustus Prew, and my wonderful parents, Scott and Nancy.

# about the author

Author photo by Dan Collopy

**Jeffery Self** is a writer, actor, and vlogger. If his face is familiar, it may be because he's appeared in numerous films and television shows, including *30 Rock*, *Desperate Housewives*, and *90210*. Or you're one of the millions of people who've viewed him on YouTube. Or you used to date him, or sit behind him in bio class. *Drag Teen* is his first YA novel.

For more about Jeffery, check him out on Twitter at @JefferySelf and online at jefferyself.tumblr.com and www.youtube.com/user /JefferySelf.